Moonlight Curse

J.L. WENNING

GYPSY PUBLICATIONS

Published in 2012, by Gypsy Publications
Troy, OH 45373, U.S.A.
www.GypsyPublications.com

Wenning, J.L.
Moonlight Curse/ by J.L. Wenning

ISBN 978-0-9842375-7-9 (paperback)

Library of Congress Control Number
2012940751

Edited by Jon Williams
Cover and Book Design by Tim Rowe
Art Director by Meaghan Fisher

PRINTED IN THE UNITED STATES OF AMERICA

I would like to thank my wife, Vickie and our two daughters, Brianna and Lauren for their patience and understanding through the process of writing this novel.

Chapter 1

Back in the late 1800s my family was on the verge of starvation when my father made a big discovery. He was out hunting one day and came home early not with food but with something in an old wooden box. He said it would change our lives forever.

My mother asked, "What is that?"

He told her, "You'll find out soon enough."

My mother went to the kettle and added the last of our cabbage to some water to make cabbage soup. Again. She told my father, "You need to go get us something to eat or this will be our last meal."

"You don't need to worry about food anymore. This will help us."

"Leon, where in the hell did you get that box, and what the hell is in it?"

"Woman, I ran into what appeared to be a witch doctor on a black horse. He traded me what was in this box for the five rabbits I shot. He told me that on the full moon all of our troubles would be taken care of."

My mother shouted, "You traded food off our table for some box that you probably have no idea of what it even is!"

"The full moon starts in two days. We will no longer starve." With that, my father left the house and headed out to the barn. My mother continued to cook the cabbage soup as my sister Ashley and I played jacks. We sat alone at the dinner table that night and ate. My mother was very irritated with my father and that made for a very quiet evening. My father was out in the barn the whole night. I was very interested in what he was doing out there, but I knew that if I let my curiosity run wild I would end up in trouble.

My father was in the barn when he decided to open the box. He pulled a skull out of the box and set it on the shelf above the workbench. I never was able to find where the box was. I was later told by my mother what the box contained. He then grabbed a flask of liquid and set it beside the skull on the shelf. He looked out at the moon.

"Only two more days until the full moon and a new start for my family," he said.

It was soon the day of the full moon. We hadn't seen much of our father for the last few days; he seemed to sleep a lot during the day and spend a lot of time in the barn at night. We had finished the last of the cabbage soup the previous day and hadn't eaten since, as my father hadn't been out to hunt. My mother finally went up in the loft to wake him up.

"Tonight, when the full moon appears, you will no longer hunger. I haven't, since I ran into that man."

My mother was frustrated when she came down from the loft. "Can you go out and try to get some food?" she asked me.

I had turned fourteen a couple of weeks before; I was almost a man. I grabbed my slingshot and headed out. I knew better then to grab my father's gun—he would tan my hide faster than a rabbit finds its hole. But no matter how hungry I was, I couldn't stop wondering what my father was doing in the barn all night.

I approached the barn, where the stench nearly knocked me over. It smelled like the butcher's shop we used to go to. I opened the barn door and looked inside. I didn't notice anything out of the ordinary, besides the stench. So I closed the door and went off to hunt. On my way out, hunting couldn't get the smell of the barn out of my nose. Something seemed different to me. We had no animals on our farm, but I knew from the smell that something had been butchered in the barn. The only place I thought of where the stench could be coming from was the old horse stall in the back of the barn. I couldn't wait to check it out. Maybe that was where my father had stashed his wooden box.

I ventured into the woods and soon made a gruesome discovery: a deer that had been torn apart. The meat was still good, but all the entrails were gone. This wasn't done by any animal native around here, I thought to myself. I took out my knife, cut some hunks of meat off the deer and put them in my rucksack, and then headed home.

When I got there, no one was in the house. I set the meat on the table and went outside, where I heard some noise coming from the storm shelter. As I unlocked the door, my mother and sister rushed out. My mother grabbed me and gave me a hug.

"We need to leave now, your father is crazy," she told me.

My father must have sensed that I had been in the barn, because he had jumped out of bed and headed out after me. When he discovered that I was no longer there, he took my mother and sister into the storm shelter and scolded them for letting me leave the house on this day. He had locked them in the storm shelter and set out to find me.

We went into the house, packed basics, and headed to the nearest town. My mother figured we had enough daylight to get there.

As we walked the path, I saw my father in the woods. My mother grabbed my sister and me by our hands and pulled us along faster. She pulled us as fast as we could go. I kept looking back, checking for my father. We had been on the move for a while when I didn't see him anymore. The hours passed as we walked. Ashley complained of her feet hurting so I gave her a piggyback.

We were about an hour away from town when I tripped and fell. My sister hit her head on the ground and I twisted my ankle. I tried to put weight on it but was unable to do so. My mother decided that we would have to camp there for the night, so she and my sister gathered some wood for a fire as I unwrapped the meat that I had in my rucksack. I crawled around to find some small sticks that I could place the chunks of meat on as they cooked.

They were off in the nearby woods, trying to scavenge up some berries. All I could think about was what would happen if they ran into my father, I was getting very nervous as I prepared the meat, I kept my eyes on the woods, looking for them to return. My mother and sister came back about twenty minutes later with wood and some water and berries. My mother started the fire, and as the meat cooked we ate some berries and drank some water. The meat was soon finished and the three of us ate. With warm food in our bellies, we turned in for the night. My sister and I both snuggled to our mother, but I had trouble sleeping. I kept thinking of the deer in the woods, how it was unlike any native animals to do that to a deer.

I was almost asleep when I was awakened by a

commotion. I felt pressure on my shoulder and then everything went dark.

Chapter 2

I woke up in my own bed with my father standing over me. "That was some fall you took yesterday," he told me.

I said, "What fall?"

"While you were out hunting you tripped and hit your head and your shoulder on a sharp rock."

I gave my father a puzzled look. He changed the bandage on my shoulder and told me to rest. He left my room and I heard his footsteps go into my sister's room. Then I heard him go up to the loft where he and my mother slept. I tried fighting the sleepiness but it was a battle that I wasn't going to win.

Later that evening I awoke and went to the kitchen. My mother, sister, and father were all sitting at the kitchen table. I noticed that my mother and sister had bandages in the same spot that I did. I started to ask my father a question when my mother spoke up.

"Your sister and I had a little incident yesterday when we were trying to help your father get you from the woods."

My stomach wasn't grumbling this evening. If my memories of what happened after I went hunting weren't true, why wasn't I hungry?

I asked my mother, "What are we having for supper tonight?"

"We're going to have a late supper tonight," she replied.

My mother and father were acting strangely, so I decided I would sneak over to Ashley's room after everyone went to bed and see what she had to say. A few silent hours passed before my sister and I were told to go to bed.

"What about supper?" I asked her.

She again just told me, "It'll be a late supper."

I just minded her and went to bed.

A few hours passed. As usual, I heard the front door open and close, so I knew the coast was clear for me to go talk to my sister. I tiptoed to her room and slowly opened her door. To my surprise, she was waiting for me.

"I figured that you'd be in to see me tonight," she said.

We talked about the events of the night before. Unless we both had the same dream, someone was lying to us and something strange was going on. We made a plan to go to the barn the next day while our father slept, to try to locate the box he had brought from the mysterious man on the black horse. My sister and I slept in the same room that night.

We slept through the morning and afternoon and into the evening. For not having anything to eat the night before, my stomach nevertheless felt full. The night was again a silent and boring one, just waiting for the sun to go down so we could be sent back to bed while my parents left the house. This kept my sister and me from looking in the barn to try to find the box

The same routine of sleeping and then just sitting at the kitchen table went on for almost a week, until finally our life seemed to return to normal. I awoke in the morning to the sound of songbirds and went out to the kitchen to find my father drinking his coffee in a good mood. My mother was cooking eggs and making tea for us. I wanted to ask were all this food came from all of a sudden, but I kept my mouth shut.

It was almost time for my sister and me to return to school. While we were both excited to go, we were also determined to enjoy the rest of our break. We ventured outside and headed to the creek to meet up with a few of our friends.

I went up to Johnny and asked him, "What are you doing?"

Johnny replied, "I'm playing fetch with my new puppy."

Just as he finished his sentence, his lab puppy brought back the stick that he had thrown for it. The puppy dropped the stick and then began to growl at me. The fur on its back stood up as it growled.

"Be quiet, Shooter!" Johnny said, but the dog wouldn't stop growling. After a few minutes, Johnny decided that he should leash Shooter up and take him home.

This just left my sister and me to play by the creek. We just enjoyed the day, taking in all the scenery and the smell of the fresh air and plants. They smelled more amazing then I remembered. We played the day away, and then it was time to go home to help with chores.

Apparently, the curse that my father had gotten us into took a while before it consumed you. The next three weeks passed quickly; before we knew it, we had started school. Everything seemed fine…until the night of the full moon.

Our parents kept Ashley and me out of school the whole week. Our teacher agreed to let our mother go over our studies with us. The week started strangely; I would go to sleep in my bed and wake up somewhere else. I didn't eat all week but I never felt hungry. The time flew by and we were able to go back to school. But when we got there, we were missing a few classmates.

I asked Mrs. Engle, "Did Johnny and Joey move?"

She informed me, "They are dead." She wouldn't tell me anything else.

I began to cry. Johnny was my best friend. We did everything together and now he was gone. I remembered the last time I saw him, playing with his new puppy, and how the puppy didn't seem to like me.

I tried to calm down. Mrs. Engle said, "I figured that your parents had told you."

"No, my parents never told me anything. They've been acting strange."

Mrs. Engle took my sister and me into the hallway. "I'll go home with you today to let your parents know about Johnny and Joey."

I tried to pay attention in school that day, but all I could think about was Johnny's puppy growling at me. I've been around a lot of dogs, and none of them ever acted that way toward me.

School finally ended for the day, and Mrs. Engle walked Ashley and me home.

My father met us on the front porch. "Leave my property," he said to Mrs. Engle.

"Mr. Johnson, I just want to know why you didn't inform your children of the tragedy that struck here last week."

"You should get going and mind your own damn business."

Mrs. Engle told us, "I'll see you two tomorrow at school." Then she walked away.

My father grabbed my sister and me by our arms and

pulled us into the house, where he called for my mother.

My mother came running and asked, "What is it, Leon?"

My father replied, "These damn kids' teacher came around, meddling in our business."

Mother looked at us. "So, what brought Mrs. Engle to our home today?"

My sister answered, "Benjamin told her you were acting funny."

I had to stop myself from hitting her. The last thing I needed was for her to start telling them everything we talked about.

"So he did," said my mother. She put her hand up to her chin as if she were trying to think of a way to punish me.

My father spoke up. "Then it is settled. We will move away from this town before people begin to get too nosy."

My mother agreed with my father, which seemed strange. Her family had lived on these grounds for almost a hundred years, just past the time of the war, and now she was easily agreeing to leave them.

Chapter 3

A week and a half passed. We had packed almost everything up. As we got ready to load the rest, the local preacher came to our house. He asked my father about donating to the church some of the things we weren't going to take with us.

My father told him, "You are welcome to whatever is left when we are gone. We aren't going to need it where we're going."

The preacher thanked my father and left.

My mother came up to my father and said, "We need to get moving. The preacher must be able to sense us."

"Don't worry about the preacher man," he replied.

We continued packing throughout the day and soon we were done. We sat down at the table and ate our last supper in the only house I had ever known. I had no clue where we were moving to or any of the events that were soon to come.

After supper, my sister and I wanted to go say goodbye to our friends but we were told not to leave the property. As we played outside instead, my dad headed to the barn for his nightly ritual. This time my mother joined him.

My sister and I began to wrestle around a little bit. She grabbed me around the neck, and as I tried to get free, the bandage covering the wound on my neck came off.

"Your neck is healed!" my sister shouted.

I looked at her like she was crazy. It hadn't been long enough for the wound on my neck to be healed already. I went up to my sister and took her bandage off; to my surprise, her wound had healed as well. This puzzled the both of us, but we had no time to let it bug us. Our parents came out of the barn and said it was time for us to turn in for the night. It was moving day in the morning.

We awoke at dawn, and to our surprise, the wagon was already loaded and ready to go. My parents must have been up all night loading it. My dad was in a great mood that morning, better than I recalled over the last month. We headed north out of town. My parents sat at the front of the wagon and my sister and I had a small space inside the wagon to play. So we played Go Fish with a deck of playing cards. Between playing cards and taking a nap, the time passed, and soon my stomach was telling me that it was time for lunch. I stuck my head out of the wagon.

"When are we stopping for lunch?"

My father answered, "Just around this bend we will stop and rest the horses."

I went back into the wagon and sat quietly while Ashley napped. About twenty minutes later, I heard my father call out to the horses, "Whoa!"

The wagon came to a slow stop. My mother stuck her head into the wagon and woke my sister up. "I need some help rounding up lunch."

I helped my father tend to the horses while my sister and mother made lunch. We took some buckets to a stream and got water for the horses.

My father said, "My arms are sore from reining the

horses. I was wondering if you could carry one of the buckets of water."

"I don't think I can carry the whole bucket of water back to the wagon," I replied.

"Yes, you can, boy. You can do more than you imagine. I need you to man up on this trip."

I picked up the bucket of water as if it were nothing. I carried it all the way back to the wagon with no problem at all. I noticed that my father never changed the arm he was carrying his with, either. I was sure he pulled a fast one on me.

When the horses were fed and watered, we sat down to eat our lunch. My sister and mother were able to forage some fresh berries to go along with some venison. With our bellies full, my sister and I climbed back into the wagon and we were off again, still heading north.

It seemed like we rode forever.

Eventually, I again heard my father call to the horses, "Whoa!"

My mother stuck her head into the wagon. "It's time for supper.

This time we had stopped close to the river so the horses could drink. My mother and sister foraged for berries while my father and I set up camp, then we went to get some firewood. My father had never let me use an axe before, but he did that night. I bonded with my father more so far on this trip then I had in my fourteen years.

When we arrived back at camp, my mother and sister had supper ready. We sat down and ate, and then gathered around the fire. I built up the bravery to ask my father, "Why have you been so secretive?"

I cringed after I asked, expecting him to yell at me. I guess the bonding we did that day may have changed him. "I'll tell you when you're ready, son."

After a few hours by the fire, the day's adventure finally caught up with all of us, and we turned in for the night. I had been asleep for a few hours when I awoke to the sound of heavy sniffing, and a warm feeling. I moved my arm and felt what I thought was fur. Convinced I was dreaming, I fell back asleep. When I awoke in the morning, I replayed the incident in my head. I mentioned it to my father, who passed it off by telling me I was dreaming.

We ate breakfast, fed the horses, and were soon on our way. I overheard my father tell my mother, "We should be there by sundown."

The excitement of reaching our destination that evening kept me wound up that day. I totally forgot about the dream I had the night before. We rode straight through that day, stopping just long enough to tend to the horses and snack on some jerky.

When we finally arrived at our destination, it was a small village. If you could even call it that— there were five or six houses and that was it. My father stopped the horses in front of a rundown house.

"Welcome to our new home."

Ashley and I looked at each other in shock. This was nothing like our other home. It looked drafty, and I wondered why my father picked this house.

We unloaded the wagon and settled in for the night. We only had some scraps of venison left and a few berries, so I went to bed hungry that night.

The next morning, my father shook me awake. He wanted me to come outside and help him. I got up out of bed and followed him outside. He handed me an axe and told me to begin to chop the wagon up for firewood.

I said, "There are plenty of trees around here. Won't we need the wagon for transportation?"

My father answered, "We won't be going anywhere, so

the wagon is no use to us."

I helped my father chop the wagon into pieces small enough to burn in the woodstove in the house. A few hours passed, and then my mother and sister came out of the house on their way to find some water and berries. My father and I had drunk all the water in the canteen while we were chopping up the wagon.

I asked my father, "Is there anyone else living here?"

"Yes, but they tend to stay to themselves. When they are ready and trust us they will meet us."

My mother and sister came back from foraging for food and water. We sat down at a makeshift table beside the house and ate. I heard some kids playing off in the woods. My father noticed that I heard them, and he reminded me, "When they are ready they will meet us."

I wanted them to hurry up. Since Johnny had died, I hadn't had much interaction with kids other than my sister.

We spent the day doing some repairs to the house. My father kept me busy helping him and my sister was busy helping my mother clean. But all the hard work made me hungry and my stomach began to growl. My father must have had good hearing, because he heard my stomach growl all the way across the room.

"Go get something to eat, son," he said.

I went to the kitchen and ate some berries and drank some water. Then I went back to work with my father. The time flew by, and soon it was time to go to bed. I was so tired from helping my father that as soon as my head hit the pillow I was asleep.

The new day brought more of the same. We worked on the house all day while my sister and mother went off to get some food. As we worked, I kept wondering when we would be able to meet the others who lived nearby. I asked my father about it again.

Again, he answered, "When they feel comfortable with us."

Even though I knew that response was coming, it still caught me off guard. I wondered how they were going to get comfortable with us if they never met us.

I continued to help my father work on the house. We again worked through the day until it was time to sleep again. That night, while I slept, I felt a weird presence with me in my room; it made me feel as if someone was watching me. I tossed and turned all night. I didn't want to wake up when my father came in to wake me up in the morning. Surprisingly, he let me sleep in.

Chapter 4

When I finally got out of bed, my father was out working and my mother and sister had returned from foraging. I went out to see if my father needed me to help him.

"Take your sister and go play," he said.

I was shocked. All three days we had been there, I heard that the people here needed to trust us, and now I could go and play. I went in the house and got Ashley.

She told me, "I thought you were going to sleep all day. Let's go play."

We went out and followed the noise of children playing. It led us into the woods and to a clearing where there was a nice play area. It had some swings, a slide, and a merry-go-round. My sister and I went and introduced ourselves to the kids.

"My name is Benjamin and this is my sister Ashley," I said to some of the kids playing.

Two of them stopped playing and introduced themselves.

"I'm Anna, and this is my brother Keith," said one of the girls.

As we played with Anna and Keith, the other kids

seemed to become more comfortable with us. Another boy came over and introduced himself.

"My name is Cody," he said.

Cody began to play with us, and soon two more girls came over and introduced themselves.

"My name is Alyssa, and this is Chrissy," one of them said.

Before we knew it, all the kids except for one older boy were all playing together.

I asked Chrissie, "Why hasn't he come over here to play?"

"He is sort of a loner. I don't ever remember him playing with any of us."

We all were having so much fun playing that we didn't even notice when it started to get dark.

Cody said, "We should all probably go home now."

I was having so much fun with my new friends that I wasn't ready to go home.

"Can't we play a little longer?" I asked.

Cody replied, "It's not a good idea to be out here after dark."

I laughed a little, but I would find out why soon enough.

We all went home. Ashley and I walked into the house, greeted by the smell of rabbit stew cooking in the kettle. My parents were both in good moods and the new house began to feel like home. We ate supper, then sat at the table and played Kings Corners with our parents.

Soon it was time to turn in for the night. I had the same feeling come over me again that night. I woke up and there was no one in my room with me, so I just shrugged it off as still getting used to sleeping in the new house.

The next day I couldn't wait to be done with my chores so I could go play with the other kids. But when we got to the play area, there were no kids there. My sister and I went back home with our heads hung low.

My father asked, "What's wrong, son?"

I moped around and answered, "There is no one to play with."

"Did you check the pond?"

"Pond? What pond?" I asked.

"The one past the clearing. All the kids are probably there," he said.

I grabbed my sister and we high-tailed it back to the clearing. We could hear the kids as we approached the pond. We ran the rest of the way, anxious to play. Cody and Alyssa met us before we got there.

"Go home!" Alyssa said.

"Why?" I asked.

"Ryan is waiting for you at the pond, and he doesn't like you," she replied.

"I never did anything to him. I haven't even said one word to him," I said.

"Just go home. We can play later," Alyssa said.

I took my sister's hand and we headed home. I couldn't understand what Ryan had against me. It would take me a few years to figure that out. After a few minutes, we arrived back home.

My father asked, "Why aren't you two playing with the other kids?"

I started to tell him when my sister interrupted. "My stomach hurts and I didn't feel like playing."

My mother took Ashley into her room. She came out less than five minutes later.

"Leon, can you come here for a minute?" Mom hollered.

"I'll be right there," answered my father. He got up from his chair and headed back to my sister's bedroom.

"What's the problem?" he asked.

My mother replied, "It's that time."

My father rolled his eyes and said, "Isn't she too young for that?"

"Leon, she is twelve years old."

"She needs to stay in the house until she is done."

My mother agreed, even though that meant she would have to do all the foraging herself.

I didn't understand what my parents were talking about at the time, but I was soon to find out.

The next day I was playing with Alyssa and Chrissie.

"Where's Ashley?" they asked.

"I overheard my mother and father say that 'it was time' and that she had to stay in for the week."

Alyssa looked at me and said, "That's why Ryan doesn't like you."

"What does my sister have to do with Ryan and myself?"

Alyssa said, "Ryan is the oldest of the boys here. He believes that he is the alpha male to be. You being close to his age threatens him."

I still didn't understand what Alyssa was talking about. I let it slide, though. We continued to play, and soon all the other kids were there. We spent the day swimming. It was soon dusk and I had to head home. On my way, the words that Alyssa spoke rang in my head. I pondered the idea of asking my parents but I decided not to. I ate supper and then it was time for bed.

I awakened in the middle of the night to the sound of a commotion outside my house. I looked out my window and saw a shadow of a person outside my sister's window. I got up out of bed and ran outside to see who it was. Ryan met me. He jumped on me and began pounding on me.

"I'm going to kill you!" he yelled.

With the way he was hitting me, he probably would have, but suddenly he was thrown off of me by one of the adults in the village.

Ryan got up off the ground and said, "It's my time, old man."

Ryan began to attack the man that pulled him off me. I was lying on the ground screaming for help. Suddenly all the adults in the village were there. Ryan and the old man battled, but no one else stepped in. The old man gained the advantage and soon the fight was over. Ryan, bloodied and bruised, limped away into the woods.

I was then tended to. I was told not to mention any of this to the children in the village; if I did, I would suffer the same consequences as Ryan. I didn't want to disrespect anyone, so I agreed.

I went back into the house and went back to bed but I had trouble sleeping that night. I had visions of what had happened flashing through my head.

I finally fell asleep. Soon, though, my father was in to wake me up.

"How are you feeling?" he asked.

"Sore, tired, and stiff," I answered.

He told me, "Just stay in bed and rest. It's going to be a long night tonight."

I didn't even think of the moon cycle for the night. I was so tired and sore I easily went back to sleep.

My father woke me in the evening.

"Son, you are going to miss the fire," he said.

"What fire?" I asked.

"All the villagers are getting together tonight for a celebration."

I got out of bed and cleaned up, then all four of us left the house. The old man that rescued me the night before met us. He accompanied us to the opening in the woods where all the other villagers were.

We had a nice fire. All of the kids played together while the adults talked around the fire. We were too far away to hear them. The time flew, and before we knew it all the kids were ordered into a building. The adults locked us in the building. All of the kids were calm except for Ashley and me. I was freaking out.

Cody came over and told me, "There is nothing to worry about. It is for our own protection."

Ashley then noticed that the others were playing cards and jacks. We realized that if the others were comfortable then we shouldn't worry. We settled down and played with them.

That whole week was the same. I grew accustomed to the sleeping late, staying up late, and somehow always waking up with a full belly despite not eating anything that I remembered. When the week was over, things went back to normal, except that we had more meat in the smokehouse then I could ever remember. There had been no sign of Ryan.

Chapter 5

That following year flew by. There was still no sign of Ryan. Ashley and I adjusted well with all the other kids. It was nearing my fifteenth birthday, and my family had a party planned for me for that Friday night. We were all gathering around to start the party when all of a sudden Ryan appeared out of nowhere. He came right after me, catching the attention of the adults in the village. They went after him, and as they did, two other guys grabbed my sister and took off.

I yelled out, "They took Ashley!"

Ryan then took off running. The adults in the village searched and searched but they couldn't find him. The old man in the village took ill. Then one night, while we were locked in the building, playing cards and jacks, we heard a crashing noise. Before we knew it, we were overcome by a pack of wolves.

I managed to escape, but I was the only one who did. I ran to the old man's house and there he was. It was Ryan, or a creature that resembled Ryan. I cringed, looking into the window as it tore the old man apart like he was a rag doll. The creature let out a bloodcurdling howl, and all the wolves came to him. Luckily I wasn't seen, and I ran off into the woods.

Once I reached the woods my senses became stronger, and I was able to track down my parents. To my dismay, they were wolves too. I stopped in my tracks and my mother and father appeared before me.

They asked, "Why are you out here?"

"Something horrible happened back at the village," I told them.

Suddenly all the men and women from the village surrounded me. I had to go into detail about what had happened.

"We were all in the building playing games as usual, when suddenly we heard a loud crashing noise, and before we knew it we were being attacked by wolves, but I managed to escape," I explained. "I ran up to the old man's house in time to see a creature that resembled Ryan tear him apart."

One of the men came up to me and said, "He killed Jack!"

"Yes, he did," I replied.

The adults huddled together for a meeting. Before I knew it, we were heading back to the village to see for ourselves. The adults split up into two groups. One group went to check the building where the children were. The other group went to old man Jack's house. I went with the group to check on the kids. The sight was horrid; the kids were torn apart. There were no survivors. The other group that went to the house soon joined us.

Ed said, "Jack's head was gone. Just his body remained."

This saddened the village. But that mood changed rapidly.

Not having an alpha male in the village led to a lot of

fighting among the men. With so much fighting, sickness and famine came to the village. I knew what I had to do, but how was I going to do it? I was only 15. The men began to drop like flies; the battles became deadly. The women had to find what they could to eat. I became distant from my father. Any of the men in the village would take me as a threat, so I stayed in hiding with my mother.

After some time, we finally had an alpha male. It was my father. Tensions calmed down in the village, but there was a problem. There were five women left, plus my mother, my father, and myself. The women left in the village were all past childbearing age. So this became a problem for our survival. My father and I took care of everyone and fended off any challenges.

The years passed, and soon it was the dawn of my eighteenth birthday. The village had survived pretty well. My father was doing a good job as the alpha male; we worked well together. But now I was turning eighteen, meaning it was time for me to leave the village and find a mate. No matter how much my father loved me, as soon as I turned eighteen the beast that lived within us would cause us to fight.

My mother sent me off early that morning. She had packed my things for me. I went off not knowing where I was going or even how I was going to survive. I didn't have enough experience on my own with my curse to find anywhere to be with people. I wandered for days, and soon the full moon came around again.

We always killed animals for our food; we never tasted the flesh of a human. So I tried to stay away from civilization. The full moon came and went with no problems. I finally was able to settle in a small village, where I got work helping the local blacksmith. I worked with the metal, not with the horses; they didn't like me too well. The apprenticeship was going well with the blacksmith and I was eventually able to get my own place.

I wanted so badly to settle down on my own but something kept nagging me to find Ryan and destroy him like he destroyed a part of me. I hadn't heard from or seen my sister in years and it was eating at me.

I asked the blacksmith, "Can I take a leave of absence? Something came up with my family and I must go back to them."

He agreed, and I was on my way to find Ryan and my sister. I traveled at night and slept through the day. I looked and searched for two weeks straight and couldn't find any trace of him. I returned to the small village after the third week and began to settle in.

One day I went to the local tavern for a drink, and I ran into a few of the local girls. They had seen me around but they didn't know who I was. I noticed one of them looking at me, so I went up to them and introduced myself.

"Hi, my name is Benjamin Reed," I said.

One of the girls shied away from me. It was the same one that had been looking at me earlier. The other two girls introduced themselves as Ginger and Emily.

Emily said, "This is Ellen. She is a little shy."

The girls and I sat under a tree and began to talk. I had to make up a story to tell them about me because I couldn't let them know the truth. I felt bad for lying to them. We sat and talked for hours and before I knew it, Ginger and Emily left, leaving Ellen with me. It was awkwardly quiet with just the two of us, neither of us knowing what to say to the other. It was beginning to get dark so I offered to take Ellen home. We walked to her house not saying a word to one another. I watched her go into her house and I headed back to mine.

On the way home, some urge came over me that I haven't felt before. I was familiar with male urges, but this was something new. My body was letting me know that it was mating time. I knew that the only way that I could see Ellen again was if I stayed away from her for a few days until her cycle ended.

I worked a lot the next few days to try to avoid Ellen and her friends. They would try to stop in and see me.

My boss told them, "He's too busy for visitors."

He came up to me later that day and asked, "What's wrong with you? You have a pretty girl calling on you and you are avoiding her."

I informed him, "I have feelings for her too, but right now isn't a good time." I used the family excuse again to keep him off my back.

Finally, the day came that Ellen was off her cycle. I was happy to see her. Along the way to meet her, I picked some flowers out of the meadow. When I arrived, she and her friends were with some other guys from town, laughing and having fun. I ripped the flowers up and stormed back to my home. It had finally caught up to me. The beast within me was now showing its teeth, the urge to protect what it saw as mine.

Chapter 6

I wandered from town to town over the next three years. I guess you could say that I was a drifter. I never stayed in a town long enough to hit the full moon. I stayed away from women, too. With my sexual desires, there was no telling what would happen.

I finally came upon a town where, for some reason, I felt comfortable. I went into the local tavern for a drink, and the server was a female. She had a scent that was very familiar to me. I had my drink and struck up a conversation with her.

She told me, "I'm off in a few hours and I would love to talk with you more after that."

I sat down and drank some water as I waited for her shift to end. After a few glasses of water and some laughs, it was time. I said goodbye to the guys I had met while I was waiting.

We took a walk off into the park. She introduced herself to me: "My name is Sarah."

"My name is Benjamin."

We sat down at a table in the park. She told me, "I live in a little village across the stream and would like it if you would come home with me."

I sensed something about her. Could she have the same curse that I did? Whatever it was, I trusted her. We headed back to her village and to her house. Her house was small and cluttered; you could tell she didn't spend much time there.

I asked her, "What is such a pretty lady doing without a man?"

"I don't need one; I can take care of myself."

"Why did you invite me home with you?" I asked.

"I can sense that you have lost something dear to you. I think I may be able to help you out."

I wondered what she was talking about. She couldn't know about my sister…could she?

Sarah could see that I was caught off guard by what she had said. "I know where she is."

I responded, "You know where who is?"

Sarah looked at me and said, "Your sister."

"Wait a minute. First of all, how do you know me, and how do you know about my sister?" I asked.

"I'll explain," she said.

"Okay, go ahead."

"Ryan is my cousin. I know it is strange, but my family is nothing like his. You asked why I don't have a husband. It's not that I don't want one; it's that he won't let me have one. This is his village, and your sister is here."

"Whoa, wait a minute! This is Ryan's village…he is the alpha male here?"

"Yes, he is, but you are safe tonight. He has the pack out hunting, and they are pretty far away," she explained.

"What are they hunting so far away?"

Sarah hesitated in her answer; she must have thought that she was already in pretty deep. Finally, though, she responded. "Ryan and his pack hunt humans."

For as long as I had the curse, I had never feasted on the flesh of a human. I couldn't believe that Ashley would stand for this, but she was young when Ryan kidnapped her. She was still young—she would only be seventeen on her next birthday.

"We have to stop them!" I shouted.

Sarah rubbed my shoulders and said, "All in time. I have a plan."

I didn't sleep much that night, knowing I was so close to Ashley, but there was nothing I could do to bring her home.

Morning came and Sarah shook me from my troubled sleep.

"We need to go," she said.

"Wait a minute! I thought you had a plan," I said.

"I did, but things changed. We need to get out of here."

Sarah and I fled from the village like rabbits running from a dog. We spent the day running. As it was getting dark, we were both hungry and tired from running. We ended up down by the river, where we were able to take shelter in a small cave along the water. I started a fire.

Sarah stomped it out and said, "What in the hell are you thinking? They will smell that fire and know where to find us."

"How will they find us? It's not a full moon. They are in human form just as we are, and this human needs to stay warm."

Sarah looked at me and said, "I'll keep you warm."

"How are you going to do that?"

Suddenly, before my eyes, Sarah changed into a wolf. She nudged my hand with her head, so I sat down, and she came up and licked me in the face. As I become more comfortable, I lay down and she snuggled against me and stood guard. I wondered how she was able to change when there was no full moon.

Luckily, morning came with no disturbances through the night. When I awoke I was surprised to see Sarah lying beside me in her human form, not the wolf from the night before. I woke her up. She stretched and turned to me.

"How were you able to change last night without the full moon?" I asked.

She replied, "Do you remember when I told you that Ryan's pack hunts humans? Well, when you feast on the flesh of a human, it makes you a mutant. If you continue to feast on the flesh, you will totally lose control over who you are. The curse will overcome you, and then you turn out like Ryan."

"So you have eaten human flesh before?" I asked.

"It was by necessity only. It was a harsh winter and there was nothing else that could sustain our pack. We began to hunt the human trappers and hunters. Believe me I'm not proud of it. That's why I'm not accepted by the pack in my own village."

I had a feeling in the pit of my stomach. I felt bad for Sarah, but I also knew that she was a killer. We were warned all the time in the village I came from that you cannot trust a killer.

I backed away from Sarah and said, "Hold it a minute!"

Sarah looked at me and said, "If I wanted you dead I could have done it last night or I could have handed you over to Ryan. I'm sure he would have enjoyed killing you like he did your parents."

"My parents? What about my parents?" I said.

"Yes, your parents. Remember those hunters and trappers I was talking about?"

"You bitch!" I yelled. "My parents! You killed my parents!"

I was going ballistic. Suddenly I felt myself hit the

ground; when I looked up I saw a snarling wolf in my face.

"Okay, I'm calm. You can heel now, Sarah," I said.

She yielded and changed back to human form. "I was denounced by the pack because I refused to take part in the massacre of the village. Remember, I only ate human flesh to survive, not to kill."

I apologized to her. "I won't judge you anymore."

We wandered around for a while as we searched for a place to settle in. I thought for a while, and suddenly I remembered the village where I used to live. I thought that I could go back to the blacksmith. Maybe he would give my job back. Maybe we could stay there.

Chapter 7

It took a few weeks to get back to the village, but we were able to make it just after the full moon. This left us with four weeks to get settled in before the next one. Sarah found work in the tavern; I went up to the blacksmith's shop.

I asked him, "Is there any way I can have my job back?"

He replied, "Yes, Benjamin, you can have your job back."

I introduced him to Sarah. He just smiled at me.

Sarah and I settled into our home, but our relationship was strange. There was no romance; we were like best friends. She would run around at night after she finished at the tavern. I would work and head home.

One day I was working at the shop when Ellen walked in. I looked up from my work and caught sight of her.

I went up to her and asked, "Can I help you?"

She looked at me and had to look again. "Benjamin?" she asked.

"Yes," I replied.

"Where did you take off to?" she asked.

"I've been here and there. How have you been?" I

asked.

"I've missed you. I saw you that day when you left. I was talking to my cousins that were in town when you were coming up the path. I tried to yell for you but you just took off."

I looked down at the ground and said, "I'm sorry."

"There hasn't been a day that's gone by that I haven't thought of you," she said. Then she grabbed me and gave me the biggest hug and kiss. She didn't seem to care that I was dirty from work.

Out of the corner of my eye, I saw Sarah come into the shop. I pushed Ellen away from me and told her that her behavior was inappropriate and that she needed to leave.

She stared at me for a moment, then stormed out of the shop. "Leave me alone, Benjamin! You're one strange person. Don't come near me again!"

"What in the hell are you doing here, Sarah?" I shouted.

"I wanted to surprise you. I haven't seen you much," she replied.

"If you weren't out running around every night then maybe we would have some time," I said.

Sarah slammed down the basket she was carrying and the food that it contained fell all over the dirty floor. The tears welled up in Sarah's eyes as she kneeled down to pick it up. I went over and kneeled in front of her. I grabbed her under her chin raised her head to look at me.

I told her, "I'm sorry. I'm confused about what you want and what's going on."

Sarah said, "I'm sorry too for being so secretive on everything. I think the two of us need to communicate a little better."

We washed off the fruit and then sat down to have lunch together. We agreed that we would talk later that night.

Sarah left the shop and headed home. I halfheartedly

worked the rest of the afternoon. I had feelings for Ellen and I knew I had probably ruined any chance that I ever had with her. I moped around the shop longer than usual that night before heading home. I walked through the door and was surprised to see Sarah there.

"Aren't you supposed to be working tonight?" I asked.

"I took the night off," she replied. "Benjamin, you need to have a seat. We need to have a serious talk."

I sat down.

She began to explain to me, "I haven't been running around at night. I've been out guarding the area. Ryan and his pack are probably still looking for us and I don't feel safe staying in one place."

She went on. "You need to calm your hormones around Ellen. Benjamin, you also need to realize that being around these humans will eventually lead to trouble. Why do you think our colonies are away from human civilization?"

I was trying to think of what to say in response but nothing came out. I really began to hate my father for what he had done to me. I no longer had a normal life, and the way my life was going, I would be on the run for the rest of it. Then I thought of it.

"What can I do about it?" I asked.

"If you want to be with Ellen you need to change her," Sarah answered.

That's the answer that I expected but I was hoping that Sarah would offer to do it for me. When she didn't, I lowered my head and headed off to bed. I wasn't there long when Sarah came into my room. I looked up at her and asked her to leave, but she didn't. She sat down on the edge of the bed and continued our talk.

"Benjamin, if I could change her for you I would, but I can't. She will not be able to take your side as the alpha female, she will always be behind me as the beta,"

Sarah explained. "You need to be strong and take care of the problem yourself, because as long as you're only able to change on full-moon nights you leave us vulnerable to attack."

I told her, "I'll think about it."

I awoke in the morning and took a detour to Ellen's house. I watched her from a distance for hours. I couldn't muster the courage to go and talk to her. I just watched until it was time for me to go to work.

When I walked into the blacksmith shop, my boss was waiting for me. "Do you feel all right?"

"I'm fine," I answered.

"Well, is everything all right at home?" he asked.

"It's really none of your business what is going on at my house!" I shouted as I threw down my hammer. "I'm going home for the day to sort out some issues."

I headed home. I just walked through the door when I heard Sarah stirring around in her room. I tried to tiptoe to mine but her hearing was too good for that. I no more then got into my room and there she was. She was sniffing the air.

"You couldn't do it, could you?" she said.

I told her, "It was harder than I expected."

"Then you're coming with me tonight. We are going to have some fun, and you can unwind."

When I asked where we were going, she never gave me a straight answer. "Just relax and try to get some rest, because we will be out all night," she said.

The hours slipped by. The more I thought about changing Ellen, the more I decided against it. I hated my life the way it was; why would I wish it onto anyone else?

Sarah came into my room at dusk. "Are you ready?"

I got up out of bed, forgetting that I was in just my

underwear. Sarah had warned me several times to stay clothed around her. When I looked at Sarah, she had a strange look in her eye. I knew I was in trouble.

"Get out of my room!" I shouted at her.

But it had no effect on her. As she came closer, I realized what it was: she was in heat and I was there. She was kissing me, but I tried to throw her off. I finally gave up fighting and let her take me down on the bed. She began to laugh.

"You're such a wimp," she said.

"What?" I asked.

"Benjamin, you're such a wimp. I'm playing with you. I ran into a couple of trappers today at the tavern and I asked them if they had any coyote-in-heat urine, and of course they did, so I put it on this towel." She pulled the towel out of her pants pocket and began to rub it on me.

The playing around piqued the interest of both of us. It eventually became a little rough and then passionate. Finally, it happened: Sarah bit me.

I gasped. Her saliva carried her mutated virus, which would react with mine. I knew the outcome would not be good.

Sarah got up. "I didn't mean to do that. I just got carried away."

I turned away from her. Suddenly, I could feel her hands on my shoulders, shaking me. When I turned around to acknowledge her, I realized I was still in bed, and she was shaking me awake. It had all been a dream.

I chased Sarah out of the room so I could get dressed, then got up and stretched. I couldn't get over how real the dream had felt. I left my room and headed out front to meet with Sarah.

Chapter 8

We headed out through the woods and to a farm. The farmer and his family were still out tending to their chores.

As we stood back, Sarah looked at me and said, "Do you smell that, Benjamin?"

I sniffed the air but didn't smell anything out of the ordinary.

"Inhale deeper," she said.

I took as deep a breath as I could. Suddenly I smelled something that I had never smelled before; I began to salivate. I couldn't figure out what it was but I liked it. Sarah looked at me and smiled. She could tell that whatever I smelled was relaxing me.

We stayed a while longer, and then we headed over to another farm. This farm was obviously different than the one we had come from. I could smell the alcohol from far away. When we got close enough we heard a man shouting, calling his wife and kids worthless. He stumbled his way out of the back door and toward us.

Sarah suddenly changed into a wolf; as he stumbled by, she attacked him. She left him lying on the ground as she changed back to human form. She came out from behind a tree and looked at me. Her mouth was covered in blood.

"Finish him off, Benjamin!" she yelled.

I cringed, but the smell of the flesh overcame my senses. I lunged for the farmer's throat and finished him off. The first taste of human flesh, as the blood ran down my face, was so exhilarating. I looked at Sarah.

She looked back and said, "How do you feel?"

I paused. "I feel wonderful."

I now had tasted the flesh of my first human prey. I now had the ability to change at will. This would provide peace of mind to both Sarah and me. I was now stronger than I had ever been, stronger than anyone in the village I came from.

"It's time," Sarah said.

"Time for what?" I asked.

"Follow me," she said.

We crept through the woods and came out into a clearing. I instantly knew where we were: I was looking right at Ellen's house. Sarah urged me to go up to the door and ask for Ellen. I hesitated for a moment. I started to the door but thought better of it. No matter the urge inside of me, I couldn't bring myself to make Ellen live the life I had.

I told Sarah, "I'm not feeling well. I want to go home."

She followed me to the house. Before we entered the front yard I began to vomit blood. I retched over and over as my stomach muscles contracted. Eventually, I was finally done vomiting.

Sarah come over to me and said, "This is the worst of it. Your stomach in human form will get used to it, and will be able to digest it."

"I don't want to eat humans," I told her.

"We only eat humans in necessity, Benjamin. We have no reason to eat humans," she explained.

"What was all that about then?" I asked her.

"He was abusive to his family. They are better off without him, and we are better off also. I guess we killed two birds with one human."

I didn't appreciate her attempt at humor, but she was right. We were better off now that I could change when I wanted, but I still struggled with the thought of changing Ellen. It would be easier if I had feelings for Sarah, but I didn't.

It took me several months to build up the courage to talk to Ellen and apologize for the way I had treated her in the blacksmith shop.

It was a nice fall evening, right around Thanksgiving, Sarah and I were out on a walk when I saw Ellen sitting on a bench in the park. Sarah nudged me.

"There she is. Go and talk to her," she said.

I looked at Ellen and noticed that she had looked back at us. I swallowed a big lump in my throat and, with some encouragement from Sarah, finally got the nerve to go approach Ellen.

"How are you doing, Ellen?" I asked.

"I thought I told you I never wanted to talk to you again, Benjamin," she said.

"I want to apologize to you for the way I acted at the shop that day. I also missed you all the time I was gone. There hasn't been a day that I haven't thought about you. I want to make it up to you."

I could see that Ellen's eyes had welled up with tears. She looked at me then she looked at Sarah. "What about her?"

"Oh, that's Sarah. She and I are just friends," I told her. Sarah then came up and joined us.

She told Ellen, "Benjamin and I are just friends. I

didn't mean to give you the wrong impression when you were at the shop, and Benjamin didn't help that out either. Benjamin has fallen hard for you."

Ellen looked at Sarah and said, "Thanks."

Ellen got up off the bench and grabbed me into a big hug. I hugged her back. Sarah walked away from us when we began to hug. I could sense some jealousy from her, but I was focused on Ellen. We sat down on the bench and talked until dark. I walked her home and then headed home myself.

Sarah met me at the door. "Did you do it?" she asked.

"Not yet," I replied.

"Why not?"

"I'm not ready yet, and I sense that you are jealous," I told her.

"Me? Jealous? Come on, Benjamin. If I wanted you I could have had you by now."

"I need to know that you are going to stick beside me in my journey to save my sister, and I'll do whatever it takes to make that happen. Rescuing my sister is the most important thing to me," I explained.

"I'll be with you, Benjamin, but you need to do right for yourself before you worry about Ashley. She may not even remember you. Ryan has her so brainwashed that she only functions to serve him and produce offspring."

"I'm so confused right now I don't know what I want," I said. "I like the way I feel when I'm with Ellen, but I don't want to make her live with this curse."

"Benjamin, you control the curse now. You have been happier since that night. That's why I made you do it. The moon doesn't control you anymore. You have the ability at all times now. You need to do what makes you happy."

I took my thoughts with me to bed that night.

The next morning when I awoke I headed to work as

usual. I was doing my job when a man came in and set a pitchfork on the counter.

"Are you able to fix this for me?"

"I sure can."

Then it hit me. I took a deep breath and noticed a familiar smell. I smelled Ellen on the man. I was jealous at first, but then I asked him a few questions.

"May I have your name, sir?" I asked.

"Chuck Wolfgang."

"Would you like me to bring it back to your farm when it's fixed?" I asked

"That would be great."

He gave me directions to his house. Even though I already knew where he lived, I listened and took good notes. He left the shop and I began to work on his tool. I worked on replacing the few tines that were broken and then headed to the farm.

I was on my way when I ran into Mandy, who was one of Ellen's friends.

"What are you doing, Benjamin?" she asked.

"I'm taking Mr. Wolfgang's pitchfork back to him."

"Are you going to talk to Ellen?" she asked.

"Maybe, if she's there," I said.

"You know she really likes you," she said.

My face blushed. "I know."

"I'll talk to you later Benjamin," she said.

"See you later," I replied.

I went on my way to Ellen's' house. Soon I arrived. I knocked on the door, which was answered by Ellen.

"What are you doing here, Benjamin?" she asked.

"Your dad was in the shop today and asked me to fix this," I replied. I showed her the pitchfork.

"If you want, you could take that to the barn for me. My father isn't home right now," she said.

"Sure," I replied.

I took the pitchfork into the barn and leaned it up against the workbench. I suddenly felt someone grab me around the neck from behind. I fell to the ground. In my panic, I bit. I didn't know who or what it was, but I bit. I ran out of the barn as fast as I could and headed home.

I walked into the house and yelled for Sarah, but she wasn't home. I just dropped to my knees put my arms over my head. "Why?" I screamed. "Why?"

I wanted to go back to Ellen's house but I couldn't muster the courage to do it. I was too ashamed. A few long hours passed and finally Sarah arrived home.

"Where have you been?" I shouted at her.

"Calm down, Benjamin. What's wrong?" she asked

"I made a delivery today to Ellen's house. I fixed her dad's pitchfork and took it back to the farm for him. Ellen asked me to put it in the barn for her, so I did. When I was in the barn, someone grabbed me around my neck. I panicked and bit whoever it was. I didn't see, because I was too ashamed to stick around," I explained.

"We need to go back there, Benjamin," she said.

"I know, but I didn't want to do it by myself," I replied.

Sarah and I waited until dark before we headed back to the farm. As we approached the farm, we noticed that all the lights were out in the house so we proceeded to go into the barn. We looked around for a few minutes. Then we saw it: a scarecrow with a bite taken out of its head.

"Great, Benjamin, you really tore him up," laughed Sarah.

I just hung my head and took all she could muster. I was just glad that it wasn't a human.

"Benjamin, I can't believe you couldn't tell you were biting on a wooden head. Didn't you get any splinters?"

I had to laugh at that one because it was true. I was so

involved in the moment I didn't realize what had happened.

"Let's get out of here," I said.

Sarah and I headed toward home, but it wasn't long before we were distracted by a howling noise in the distance. After we heard it a second time, Sarah and I went to investigate. We headed deep into the woods but didn't find anything. Eventually we wrote it off as a stray dog, and headed home.

Chapter 9

For the next few nights, Sarah acted strangely. I knew it was from the previous events of the week that had her so jumpy and nervous. She was gone again all hours of the night, coming home in the morning exhausted. We didn't talk much that week. I knew she was growing impatient for me to make my decision and grow our pack. I was just waiting for the perfect time.

The weekend finally came and it was time for the big Fall Harvest Festival. Everyone from the village was there, and the adults were enjoying the whiskey more than they should. This was the opportunity I was looking for.

"Would you like to go for a walk, Ellen?" I asked.

"Sure," she replied.

We walked into the woods, finding a path that led into a meadow. I pulled out a blanket.

"Would you like to sit with me and look at the stars?" I asked.

"That sounds like an idea," Ellen replied.

We sat on the blanket gazing up at the stars. It was very romantic, and the first time I hadn't screwed anything up with Ellen. I wanted to change her, but I couldn't do it. We sat and enjoyed the stars until it was time for her to leave. I walked her back to her house. On the way, she kept complaining of her foot feeling as if it was on fire. I thought nothing of it. I hugged her at her gate and watched her go into the house. Then I headed back home.

I wasn't long before I heard Ellen's father running through the village. "Where is Dr. Morris? I need him!" he yelled.

Doctor Morris stumbled out of his house, half drunk.

"I'm right here. What do you need?" he said.

Ellen's father ran to him. "It's Ellen. She was stung by a bee, and she is having trouble breathing," he said.

Sarah joined me on the front porch. "You know what you need to do, Benjamin. You are the only hope she has. Doc Morris isn't a great doctor when he is sober."

Finally, it seemed the time had come. I ran over to Ellen's farm as fast as I could. I got there just in time. I could hear her struggling for every breath she took.

"Can you leave us alone for a moment?" I asked Ellen's mother.

She hesitantly agreed and stepped out of the room. As soon as she was gone, I sank my teeth into Ellen's neck and shoulder area long enough to let my saliva mix into her bloodstream.

"You'll be fine now," I told her as I left the room.

Her mother stopped me as I was leaving the house. "Is she going to be okay?" she asked me.

"She will be in a few days. Just let her rest," I told her.

I went back to the house, where I was met by Sarah. "Did you do it?" she asked.

"I had to. She was going to die if I didn't."

"We need to get her out of the house and over here," she said.

"I know we do. Let's wait until morning, then we will

go over there and talk to her parents."

"Are you that stupid, Benjamin? Talk to her parents? We need to go get her tonight!"

"Just calm down, Sarah. I've already got a plan," I said.

"I don't know about this, Benjamin. If your plan doesn't work we need to do mine," Sarah demanded.

Morning came, and it was time to head to Ellen's house. I went over and was greeted by her father.

"What brings you by, Benjamin?" he asked.

"Just curious how Ellen is doing this morning," I said.

"She is doing a lot better than last night, thanks to you. Whatever you did to her has made a great improvement in her. She seems very strong."

"Yes, speaking of last night, I have a question for you," I said.

"What's that, Benjamin?" he asked.

"I would like to ask you for permission to marry your daughter."

"Well, let's see. You have a good job. You seem like a fine young man, and I know that she is madly in love with you. You have my permission," he said.

I was pleased with his quick answer, but I also needed to convince him to let me take Ellen to my house to heal.

"I was wondering one more thing, Mr. Wolfgang." I said.

"What is that, Benjamin?"

"I would like to take Ellen back to my house to take care of her. You have the farm and other children to take care of. My friend Sarah and I can help her get back to normal."

He thought it over. "Okay, Benjamin, you take Ellen back to your house to take care of her. My wife has been sick recently and this would take a load off her shoulders, so she can get feeling better," he replied.

We made plans to get Ellen to my house. He went into the house and let his wife know the news. She was ecstatic that I had asked for Ellen's hand in marriage.

I went back to my house. Sarah met me at the door.

"So what's going on?" she asked.

"She'll be here later today," I answered.

Sarah went out to the woods to gather some herbs and other things we would need to help Ellen transform. Sarah was nice enough to share her room with Ellen, so I prepared it for her arrival. The time flew by. Sarah came back from the woods with what she had gathered.

"This should do it," she said.

I went over to the table to check what she had gathered and noticed many of the same things that my father had stashed in the barn all those years ago.

"Whoa!" a voice called from outside.

It was Ellen's father. He had arrived with Ellen. I went out and met him at the wagon. We helped Ellen down off the wagon and showed her into the house. Sarah stayed with her in the bedroom as her father and I unloaded her belongings from the wagon.

"You know that we are breaking the beliefs of our religion, letting her move in with you before you are married," he said.

"I know, and I promise you that as soon as she is up to it we will marry," I told him.

"I know you will. We will cross that bridge when the time comes."

I thanked him for bringing Ellen. He turned around and headed back to his wagon.

I went back in the house, where Sarah was tending to Ellen.

"How is she doing?" I asked Sarah.

"She is doing fine, Benjamin. She'll be as good as new in a few days."

I realized that the full moon cycle began in a few days. Ellen would be at the mercy of the full moon; she would be healed by its light.

Chapter 10

The weeks passed. Ellen was doing well with the whole situation. We were planning our wedding. Ellen was very happy, her mother was feeling better, and the two of them spent a lot of time preparing for the wedding. Everything was going well until it happened.

It was the week before Ellen and I were to marry when the big snowstorm hit us. We got 36 inches of snow out of nowhere. The village shut down completely; we barely had enough food to feed everyone. Sarah and I contributed as much food as we possibly could without being detected by the hunters that were out almost around the clock trying to scrounge up food. We knew that the first sight of wolves in the area would start an outcry since everyone was looking for food.

The winter was very cold and harsh. People were beginning to starve. The whole village was on edge when, finally, a discovery was made that changed everything. Three villagers were out in the woods hunting when they found an unfamiliar animal. Not knowing what it was, they brought it back to the village. Sarah knew what it was right away and it didn't take me long to smell the death on it. It was a lycan.

A lycan was a werewolf, but of a certain type. They were not picky about what they ate and included humans in their regular diet. They also were a stronger, more evil breed of animal than Sarah or myself. They had less human feeling and more animal instinct. All I knew was that this could mean definite trouble for the already starving village. With one lycan found, there had to be more in the area. We hurried and burned the body so no others could track it.

A week went by and the weather hadn't let up any. Sarah and I did all we could to help the village. People were growing sicker and weaker by the day, but their sickness wasn't from starvation. Something else was causing it. Sarah, Ellen, and I had a meeting to discuss how we could handle the situation.

"Are you ready to lead a pack, Benjamin?" asked Sarah.

I was only 21 years old. I was in no way ready to lead a pack, but I didn't have much choice if I wanted the village to survive.

The night of the full moon approached, and what happened that night changed the village forever. We changed everyone that was still healthy enough that night; the rest we had to let die. I now was the leader of a pack. I now had the ability to track down Ryan and find my sister.

The winter passed, and Ellen and I were married. There was a big ceremony. Her mother was proud of her, and her father accepted me into their family, even though he didn't have much of a choice. Sarah had taken some of the villagers with her to track down where Ryan and his pack were hiding.

Everything was back to normal at the village. We blended in well with all the new villages that popped up throughout the spring. More and more people were moving to the area.

Springtime came, bringing planting season for the villagers. We planted many herbs that we needed along with the usual corn and other crops. While I was out hunting, I met a man from a neighboring village who told stories of horseless carriages on the east coast. I was intrigued by his stories and so I invited him back to the house for supper.

We invited some of the villagers over as well and we all listened to the man, whose name was Martin. He told of the horseless carriage and many other happenings from the east coast. We all had a great time until it was time for Martin to head back to his village. We told him not to be a stranger.

Sarah arrived back at the village along with the others.

"No sign of them anywhere," she said.

"What do you mean, no sign of them?" I asked.

"Their village has been abandoned, it looks like possibly just the past winter," she said. Then she added, "Benjamin, do you remember the smell on the lycan the hunters brought here?"

"I do, but what does it have to do with them leaving their village?" I asked.

"Do you remember how our villagers were showing signs of sickness not related to starvation? Ryan's pack must have attacked a neighboring village infected by the plague," she said.

"Are you saying that the lycan that was brought here may have been from Ryan's pack?" I asked.

"It's a possibility," she answered. "But we checked for hundreds of miles all around and there was no sign of them anywhere."

Our conversation made me uncomfortable. Luckily we had burned all the bodies that had died in the village and didn't consume any of them. But I was still uneasy about the possibility of the lycan being one of Ryan's. We stepped up the security in our village. I also asked Martin if he would report any unusual sightings to me.

That year went by so fast, and before I knew it I was informed that I was going to be a daddy. This excited me very much. Ellen informed me that she was due right around Thanksgiving. That was the bad part of it: if we were hit again with snow like the year before, the extra mouth to feed could be detrimental. All I could do was hope for the best. Our harvest was great; we had plenty of food in the newly built smokehouses and things were looking good.

Then the day came that I was waiting for. Ellen's mom came and told me that Ellen was in labor. I went to our bedroom where she was to deliver. I held her hand as she went through the contractions. After a few hours, he appeared, the most beautiful gift a wife could give to her husband. He had all ten fingers and toes, and boy could he cry. We named him Jason.

As the winter passed, Jason grew like a weed. He occupied any free time that I had. Sarah was like his second mother; the kid never starved for attention. Having Jason in my life made me miss Ashley more. Her absence left a void in my heart that I couldn't fill. I knew Ellen could sense that I was missing something.

"Benjamin, why don't you go find her? We'll be fine here at the village," she said.

It was very tempting, but that would leave my family unprotected. If anything happened to either of them, I wouldn't be able to live with myself.

"I don't want to leave you here until I know you're safe," I told her.

Sarah must have been listening because she came into the kitchen. She said, "Benjamin, you have a family now. Even though you treat me as family, I really have no purpose here. Let me look for Ashley again. It will get me out of here and make me feel useful again."

I understood were she was coming from, because ever since Ellen and I got married she had been like a third wheel. I agreed to let her take three villagers and search for Ryan and Ashley.

"We'll leave first thing in the morning," she said.

I don't think I got any time with Jason that night; his aunt Sarah spoiled him with her attention instead.

Morning arrived and Sarah was off. I hugged her and told her thank you. She gave Jason a kiss goodbye and told him that she loved him. Jason cried a lot that morning, Ellen and I did everything we could but he missed his aunt Sarah.

Chapter 11

Sarah and the others had been gone for several days when they stumbled upon a new village. It was just being constructed.

"Where you from?" a voice said to Sarah.

Sarah looked around and she noticed a man painting the new general store.

"I'm a drifter," she told him

"You're a drifter. I'm not buying that story. You're much too pretty to be a drifter," he said.

"Is there any place to get a bite to eat around here?" she asked.

"There is a little restaurant around the corner. If you can wait a few minutes I'll join you," he said.

Sarah went back to the others. "You three look around. I'm going to see what I can pry out of this guy," she said.

The others went about their business checking out the new village and Sarah went to lunch with the painter.

"So, beautiful, what is your name?" he asked.

"My name is Carrie. What's your name?" Sarah asked.

"My name is Brian," he said.

"How long have you been in this village, Brian?" asked

Sarah.

"Just a few months. I was passing by and heard through the grapevine that someone needed a painter. So that's why I was painting the general store."

"So where did you live?" asked Sarah.

Brian replied, "I came from a village that is about a three-week hike from here. The food supply mysteriously began to disappear. Then a few of the villagers had a run-in with some mysterious creatures."

"What? Stop for a minute!" shouted Sarah. "Can you describe to me what the villagers saw?"

"It walked on two legs and looked like a cross between a human and a dog," he answered.

"Would you be able to take my friends and me back to that village?"

Brian replied, "There is no way in hell that I'm going back there, and you would be stupid if you did."

He got up from the table and headed toward the door. Sarah followed him. She was almost to the door when she realized that she needed to pay for her food. She went up to the bar and paid for her meal and then she headed back to the general store to find Brian.

"Why are you so interested in those creatures?" asked Brian.

"It's a long story. I'll tell it to you sometime, but you must let me know the way to that village," answered Sarah.

"Okay. You go east of town here. You probably should stay and rest, though. It is a tough three-week hike from here. Unless you could manage to get some horses and a wagon from one of the villagers."

Sarah replied, "Horses and I don't get along very well. We will be hiking the whole way."

"You better get some rest then," replied Brian as he got back to painting the general store.

Sarah went back to meet with the others. She sat down with them.

"We have a long journey ahead of us," she told them. "The gentleman that I talked to in the village explained to me that he came from a different village. He told me that his village became deserted because of the lack of food."

"So what does that have to do with us?" asked Elizabeth.

Sarah went on to explain, "The villagers came back from hunting reporting sightings of a creature that walked on two legs and looked like a cross between a human and a dog."

"A lycan," Laura said.

"Yes, lycans," replied Sarah. "We need to get a good night's rest since we have a long journey ahead of us."

Charles spoke up. "Can't we just trade Laura for some horses and a wagon?"

Sarah chuckled. "Charles, you're an idiot. You know how horses and I get along, anyway."

Charles just laughed it off.

Sarah reminded them, "It's only a few more days until the full moon, and we'll be able to travel faster through the night."

They went to the local bed and breakfast and checked in for the night.

As morning approached, Sarah was awakened by a vision. She saw Ellen struggling with someone or something, but the vision was too cloudy for her to make out what exactly it was. The vision concerned Sarah because she hadn't had one since she was under Ryan's control and living in his village.

Sarah got up out of bed, cleaned up, and met the others downstairs for breakfast. They all ate a good breakfast, checked out, and began their journey.

Sarah and the others were making good time on their hike. Suddenly Sarah heard some noises coming from far behind them. As the noises got closer, she recognized them as the sound of horses. Suddenly she heard a familiar voice call out, "Carrie!" Sarah turned around to see Brian in the wagon calling to her.

Sarah called out to the others, "Wait up."

Sarah and the others waited for Brian to come up to them in the wagon. As soon as the horses smelled Sarah, they began to act up.

"Told you horses don't like me," Sarah said.

"Oh, I know, but I figured I'd help you guys back to the village after all," replied Brian.

Sarah thanked Brian and introduced him to her friends.

"This is Elizabeth, this is Laura, and this is Charles," she told him.

"My name is Brian. It's a pleasure to meet you all," he said. "Using the wagon will cut the travel time in half, and it will also give us shelter through the night."

Sarah and the others crawled into the wagon and they set off again.

"What are we going to do, Sarah?" asked Laura.

"We'll figure something out. It's still two more weeks until the full moon, and Brian said taking the wagon should cut our time in half. With the way this wagon is packed, we won't have to look for food, at least."

Sarah stuck her head out the front of the wagon to talk to Brian.

"Why are you doing this?" she asked.

"Because I want to," he replied.

"You acted like you wanted nothing to do with going back to your old village when we talked over lunch yesterday."

"I know. I thought it over all night, and, as you can tell

from the way the wagon is packed, I didn't sleep at all. I just didn't want you to have to go alone," he said.

"But I'm not alone," she answered.

"I know, but there is just something about you that drives me nuts."

Sarah looked at Brian and said, "When we stop for the night, you and I need to talk."

Before Brian could say another word, Sarah pulled herself back in the wagon with the others.

"What's going on, Sarah?" asked Laura.

"Oh, nothing," replied Sarah.

Elizabeth spoke up. "We know something is bothering you, Sarah, and you might as well tell us."

"All right. Brian told me that something about me drives him nuts," said Sarah.

"So?" replied Elizabeth.

"What do you mean, 'so?'" shouted Sarah. "He doesn't know anything about me. He thinks my name is Carrie."

"We can't let him find out our secret," added Charles.

"We need him for the journey, so I think we need to be honest with him," Sarah said.

"I think Sarah likes Brian," Elizabeth said.

Sarah put Elizabeth in to her place by saying, "Stop being so immature. You know that I'm only loyal to Benjamin and Ellen. They are my family, just as they are all of yours. Bringing a human into our situation for any reason besides the good of the village or for the good of Benjamin and Ellen would be unacceptable."

"I'm sorry," replied Elizabeth.

There was little more said for the rest of that night, until a "Whoa!" broke the silence.

Sarah put her head through the front of the wagon to see why Brian was slowing the horses.

"This looks like a good place to stop," he said.

Sarah got the others up and moving. They all got out of the wagon and stretched. Charles and Brian went out to find some wood for a fire. The girls began to open a crate that contained the food. Sarah opened another of the crates. She looked at its contents.

"What the hell is this?" she asked.

Elizabeth looked into the barrel. "It looks like meat, but why is it so salted?"

"I don't know, but I hope he has a lot of water to wash all this salt down," Sarah said.

Laura and Elizabeth laughed at Sarah's comment. Just then, the men returned with the firewood.

"Well, it looks like we won't need that to cook anything in here," said Sarah.

Brian looked at Sarah with a puzzled look on his face. He then noticed the box on the ground beside Sarah.

"Don't touch that!" he shouted.

Sarah looked at him. "Why not? Isn't this our food?"

"Not that! Just don't touch it," he replied. He snatched the meat from her. He then placed it back in the box and placed the box under another box.

"This is what we eat," he told Sarah as he handed her a different box.

Sarah opened the box and found assorted dried fruits, peanuts, and raisins.

"What a coincidence: trail mix while we're on the trail. I guess this will do, even though I'm sort of a meat eater myself," she said.

They all five sat down and ate.

When they had finished eating and were beginning to settle in for the night, Brian came up to Sarah. "So, do you want to talk?" he asked.

"Later," Sarah answered.

Brian went and sat on a log by himself as the others

began to turn in for the night. A few hours had passed when Brian felt someone touch him on the shoulder. He turned and saw that it was Charles.

"What are you doing here by yourself?" asked Charles.

"Carrie was supposed to come out here and talk to me. She said that she needed to explain something to me," replied Brian.

"Who's Carrie?" asked Charles.

Brian gave Charles a dumbfounded look. Charles then remembered what Sarah had said to them in the back of the wagon earlier.

"Oh, what was I thinking? Carrie is already asleep," Charles said.

Charles knew that he had screwed up. He left Brian at the log and headed over by the fire to turn in for the night.

Sarah awoke in the middle of the night. She got up and looked around and saw that Brian was nowhere to be found. She looked in the back of the wagon and noticed that the box that Brian had taken from her earlier was gone. She decided that she should go out and investigate.

She ventured out a few hundred yards around the camp and still couldn't locate him. She decided to head back to the campsite. When she arrived and found Brian sleeping on the seat on the front of the wagon, she tried to tell herself she had missed him before and overreacted. She went back to sleep.

Too soon, she felt someone nudging at her shoulders. "Wake up, Sarah, it's time to go," the voice said.

Sarah slowly opened her eyes and saw Laura kneeling beside her. "What time is it?" she asked.

"Past dawn," replied Laura.

Sarah got up and prepared herself for another full day of travel. She didn't mention the previous night's events. She didn't want to overreact again.

The first part of the day's travel was silent. Eventually Brian stuck his head into the wagon.

"We need to water the horses, so we'll be stopping here for a while."

Sarah looked at Brian. "What do you mean by 'a while'?" she asked.

Brian offered no response, so she hopped out of the back of the wagon and headed toward the front to confront him. He was already on his way to the stream to get water for the horses. Sarah followed him.

"Why are we stopping?" she asked. "We went the whole day yesterday without stopping to water the horses. Why are we stopping now?"

"This is the last watering hole that amounts to anything for a while. So we need to let the horses drink and store what we can," he replied.

Sarah felt like an idiot for suspecting something was up after Brian's explanation. "I'm sorry," she told him.

Brian replied, "You need to trust me, and I need to be able to trust you. So when are we going to have that talk?"

"Tonight."

Sarah went back to the others while Brian tended to the horses. She had just arrived back at the wagon when she was approached by Laura.

"So why did we stop?" Laura asked.

"Brian said that this is the last large watering hole for awhile. So he wanted to let the horses rest and drink their fill while we work on storing some water," answered Sarah.

The four of them sat down and ate. They were finishing up when Brian came up to them.

"Charles, can you help me load some water onto the wagon?" he asked.

"Sure, but where are we going to put it? It's already a little cramped in the wagon."

"Then Carrie can ride up front with me."

Sarah looked at Elizabeth and motioned her over. "You sit up front with him," she whispered.

"I don't feel comfortable with him," Elizabeth whispered back.

"Just do it!"

Sarah approached Brian as he and Charles finished loading the water. "Elizabeth will ride with you on the front of the wagon," she told him.

Brian looked at Sarah. He said no words, but his stare pierced right through her. Sarah wasn't going to back down; she stared right back at him. Brian turned to finish harnessing the horses, and soon they were back on their way.

Sarah gathered Charles and Laura in the back of the wagon. She didn't want Brian to hear them over the clip-clop of the horses' hooves.

"I don't know about you two, but something is really bothering me about Brian," Sarah said.

"I think he is all right," replied Charles.

Laura spoke. "I don't know what it is about him, but I sense something about him that makes me feel uncomfortable."

"Well, what do you think we should do?" asked Sarah.

"I don't feel like a three-week hike," replied Charles.

"He knows where we're going, so even if we leave him he will be able to find us," added Laura.

"I know, but..." Sarah sighed. "Last night while we slept, I got up in the middle of the night. Brian was nowhere to be found. I looked all around, but there was no sign of him. When I came back to the campsite, he was asleep in the front of the wagon. I swear he wasn't there when I checked earlier." She paused. "I may be overreacting."

"I don't think you are," Laura said.

"Let's just give him a chance," replied Charles.

The three of them continued their discussion. Before they knew it, evening was approaching and it was soon time to stop.

After the wagon stopped, Sarah went right over to Elizabeth.

"Did he say much?" she asked.

Elizabeth replied, "No, he really didn't talk much, but I did notice him looking over his shoulder to the side behind us."

"Carrie!"

Sarah and Elizabeth cut their conversation short. Sarah went over to Brian.

"Are you ready for that talk yet?" he asked.

"All right. First of all, my name isn't Carrie, it's Sarah. Second, what is the real reason you changed your mind about this trip? Last but not least, what is in those boxes that you are protecting?"

Brian answered, "Like I told you before, I was up all night pondering my decision not to go. I decided to go because something about you drives me nuts, and I don't know what it is. If you would have ridden up front with me you would know that we are not alone. We are being followed. I use the salted meat to keep them from eating us."

"What do you mean, we are being followed?" asked Sarah.

"Mountain lions. We are being followed by mountain lions," replied Brian.

"Do you think I'm stupid?" asked Sarah. "There aren't any mountain lions around here."

"Fine. Tomorrow you ride up front with me, and you'll see," replied Brian.

Sarah stormed away from him. She went over to Laura

and Elizabeth.

"He must think I'm stupid or something. He told me he has the salted meat to keep mountain lions from following us," she told them.

Elizabeth replied, "I told you he kept looking off to the side of the wagon like he was watching something."

"Well, I'm riding up front with him tomorrow, and I'll keep my eyes open," Sarah said.

Laura went into the back of the wagon to do a little investigating of her own. She started unstacking some of the crates that the mysterious boxes had been hiding under.

"Don't even think about it!" a voice shouted at her.

She turned around. To her surprise, it was Charles shouting at her. He grabbed her by the arm and pulled her out of the wagon. He then dragged her to Sarah.

"Release her, Charles!" shouted Sarah.

Charles tossed Laura to the ground. "She is up to something, Sarah!" he shouted.

This angered Sarah. "Explain your theory, Charles," she said.

"I found her in the back of the wagon, going through our boxes of supplies. I think she is trying to poison us."

Before Sarah could get a word out, Brian came up to them. "It's been a long journey. You all have been cooped up in the back of the wagon for hours and hours. Let's get a good night's rest, and maybe only travel for half the day tomorrow," he said.

Sarah replied, "That sounds like a good idea."

The girls and guys split up for the night.

Chapter 12

Charles and Brian found a log in the woods, sat down upon it, and began to talk.

"Charles, why do you let Sarah boss you around?" asked Brian.

"I don't know. I guess it's always been like that since after last winter," answered Charles.

"What happened last winter?"

"Well, prior to last winter, Sarah and a man came to our village. They were outcasts from another village and were very secretive. Then the guy took a liking to one of the girls from our village. They were out for a walk in the meadow when a bee stung her. She must have been allergic or something. This guy told her family that he could save her if he could have their permission to marry her, and they gave their permission."

"What does any of that have to do with last winter?" asked Brian.

"Let me finish," replied Charles. "We had a very hard winter. Food was scarce. Some of our hunters brought back an animal that they had found dead. Sarah referred to it as a lycan. Suddenly people began dying in the village of what

Sarah referred to as a plague. The lycan was burned. Most villagers, myself included, became weak from starvation. Then one morning we woke up and everything was fine. Now we all obey Sarah and Benjamin."

"Who's Benjamin?" asked Brian.

"He is the stranger that came to the village with Sarah. The whole village praises him for saving us," answered Charles.

"Interesting," replied Brian. He stood and stretched. "I'm going to turn in for the night." He headed toward the wagon.

Sarah was fighting sleep, trying to keep an eye on Brian. She watched him vigorously as he returned from the woods, but all he did was go right to the wagon and lay down on the bench. She couldn't keep her eyes open any longer and she fell asleep.

She hadn't been asleep for very long when in the distance she heard a noise. She got up and ran away from the campsite. She took her wolf form and went in search of the noise's source. She searched all around the area several times but still couldn't find anything. She changed back to human form and headed back to the campsite, where everyone was accounted for and asleep. The noise puzzled her. Maybe she had just been dreaming. She lay back down and fell asleep.

Sarah and the others were awoken in the morning by the sounds of birds chirping. Everyone ate around the fire. Afterward, they voted on the whether they wanted to rest half the day or travel the whole day. The only one who objected to traveling only half the day was Sarah. She wasn't comfortable in the area because of what she had heard the night before, and she was very anxious to get to the village. She was a good sport, though. She didn't complain about loafing around all morning. She used the time to freshen up and write in her journal.

April 23, 1895, Last night I was awoken by a strange sound. I went out to investigate the sound, but I couldn't find anything. It's been strange since we ran into this man Brian. I've begun having visions again. I haven't had visions since I was under Ryan's control. The thing that is so strange is that my visions aren't clear. I don't know if I trust Brian completely, but riding in a wagon sure beats travel on foot, be it two feet or four. The stress of the trip is taking a toll on all of us. Just yesterday Charles said that Laura was trying to poison our food. What will happen next on our adventure? I miss Benjamin, Ellen, and Jason tremendously every day. This whole journey is for them. They gave me a family that Ryan took away.

Sarah had just closed her journal when Laura came up to her.

"I was trying to find out what was in those boxes yesterday when Charles attacked me," she said.

"I know that you wouldn't do anything to harm us, Laura," replied Sarah. "But Charles has been acting strangely lately."

The two of them chatted for a little while longer before they were interrupted.

"It's time to go!" shouted Brian.

They all loaded into the wagon. Instead of Sarah riding up front with Brian, he requested that Charles ride with him.

They traveled the whole day through without stopping. Brian was very quiet the whole time. As soon as evening set in, he stopped the horses for the night. They all got off the wagon, tended to the horses, and ate. Brian and Charles kept to themselves and the girls did likewise. Sarah was having doubts about Brian, but she needed to focus on her mission.

They all turned in early that night, except for Sarah. She stayed up most of the night trying to focus on her surroundings. She fought sleep as long as she could, but soon she lost the battle.

Several long and quiet days of travel passed. Finally the silence was broken by Brian.

"One more day," he said.

Sarah was excited about getting so close. She went off into a meadow and took the last fifteen minutes of daylight to write again in her journal.

April 29, 1895: The tension in our travel party could be cut with a knife. The men have excluded the women from nearly everything. This has been the quietest part of the journey. I'm worried about Charles; Brian seems to be changing him. Charles used to be very outgoing and fun to be around. He has become withdrawn and quiet around us. I have to keep picturing Jason and remembering that I'm doing this for him. I wish I could be holding him right now. I really miss him. Brian said one more day of travel. We are so close but with the tension…are we ready? I hope that we are on the right track and somehow we can make it through this and still have our friendships when we're done.

Sarah made it back to the campsite and gathered everyone around the fire. "We need to come up with a plan," she said.

"Let's split up," replied Charles. "We'll be able to cover more ground if we do."

"That sounds like a good idea," Sarah said, "but I'm going with Brian."

"I would rather not go with you, Sarah," replied Brian. "I'll go with Charles."

This upset Sarah. She already felt as is the women were being secluded from Brian and Charles on the trip.

"Whatever you two want to do. You two make a plan and we'll follow it," she said.

She gathered Laura and Elizabeth away from the fire.

"I don't like this one bit. We need to leave tonight by foot," she told them.

"But it's not a full moon," replied Laura.

"Remember what Brian said," Elizabeth said.

"Do you two actually believe him?" asked Sarah.

"No, but I don't want to chance it," replied Laura.

"Fine!" Sarah shouted. Then she took off.

Laura and Elizabeth waited about an hour for Sarah to return. When she didn't, they headed back to the fire. They explained to Charles and Brian that Sarah had taken off.

"She'll be back," replied Charles.

"I'm not looking for her tonight. We'll look in the morning if she isn't back by then," Brian said.

Laura and Elizabeth went to the wagon to gather their sleeping gear, then headed back to the fire to lie down. They thought Sarah would be fine on her own. By now she had probably changed and would be well on her way toward the village.

The men sat by the fire. Brian went to the wagon, coming back with a glass bottle. He took a big swig from it and handed it to Charles.

"What is it?" asked Charles.

"Corn whiskey," replied Brian.

Charles took a big swig of the corn whiskey. "Man, that's good," he said.

Brian and Charles took turns chugging the whiskey. It wasn't long before both of them were drunk.

"Charles, you're becoming a good friend, yet I hardly know anything about you," Brian said.

Loosened by the alcohol, Charles began to spill his guts.

"I already told you about my village, but I left out the good part. I'm a shape shifter."

"Wait a minute. You're a what?" asked Brian.

"A shape shifter," answered Charles.

"I have no idea what you are talking about."

"Basically, I'm a werewolf."

"You're kidding me, right?" laughed Brian.

"No, sir. We all are. That's why we are so interested in the animals your hunters saw at your village," answered Charles.

Brian looked over at the girls sleeping.

"Prove it to me," he said.

"I can't until it's a full moon," answered Charles. "But Sarah can change at will."

Brian got up and headed over to the girls. He grabbed Laura by the arms and shoved them up above her head. Before she was able to wake all the way up, Brian began ripping at her clothes. Elizabeth got up and tried to defend her, but Brian was able to fend her off with one arm.

"Charles, help!" yelled Elizabeth.

Brian continued to assault Laura. He ripped off all her clothes and began to assault her sexually.

Charles stumbled over, but he was too intoxicated to be much help. Elizabeth kept throwing punches at Brian, to no avail. She and Charles together were still no match for Brian. Exhausted, Elizabeth finally left the camp area

He finally finished with Laura and set his eyes on Elizabeth. As he approached, Elizabeth mustered the strength to get up and run away. Brian was too worn out to chase her, He turned to Charles and pummeled him. As he headed back to the wagon, he kicked Charles in the head, knocking him out cold. Then he climbed up in the wagon and left.

About thirty minutes later, Elizabeth returned to

the campsite. She noticed the wagon was gone. From a distance, she called for Charles.

"How's Laura?" she yelled.

Getting no response, she tried again. Again, there was no response. Elizabeth made her way closer to the campfire and noticed Laura curled up in the fetal position. Elizabeth knelt beside her.

"How are you?" she asked.

Laura replied, crying, "I knew we couldn't trust him. I can't believe he did this to me."

"I know," replied Elizabeth.

Laura managed to get up out of the fetal position. She buried herself in Elizabeth's chest and cried. Elizabeth ran her fingers through Laura's hair to try to calm her.

"Everything is going to be fine, honey," she told her.

Laura looked at her for a moment, and then she re-buried her head in Elizabeth's chest. The two of them held each other through the night. Elizabeth barely slept that night, keeping her eyes open to see if Brian would return.

Chapter 13

Morning had come and Sarah had woken up. She was still very frustrated about the previous night's discussion with Laura and Elizabeth. As she looked around, she couldn't make heads or tails of where she was or even how far she had strayed from the camp.

"Damn it!" she shouted.

Sarah knew that her temper had let everyone down. She knew that the only way she would have a chance to make it up to them was to somehow find her way back to them.

Charles woke up slowly. He had to shake cobwebs out of his head. He gave his eyes time to focus, then he noticed that the wagon was gone. He looked around the campsite and saw Elizabeth and Laura curled together. He stood up and walked over toward the girls.

Laura saw Charles coming over to them and hid behind Elizabeth. Elizabeth was just waking up.

"Wait a minute, Charles!" shouted Elizabeth.

"What happened last night?" asked Charles.

"You don't remember?" Elizabeth shot back.

He thought for a second. "No. I had way too much of that corn whiskey. I'm surprised I even woke up."

"Brian raped Laura. The way your face looks, he must have done a number on you also. Then he took off. Sarah hasn't returned yet. I have no clue how to get where we are going, or even how to get back to our village."

Charles took off his shirt and handed it to Elizabeth. "Have Laura put this on," he said.

Laura took the shirt from Elizabeth and put it on, then came out from behind her.

"Are you okay?" Charles asked her.

"I'll be fine," answered Laura. "We need to find Sarah."

"We should wait here until she returns," Charles said. "I'll find some timber to make shelter while you two gather food."

Meanwhile, Sarah was still trying to gather her senses and figure out where she was. She still had no clue how she was going to get back to camp. She decided to change back to a wolf and try to retrace her tracks from the night before.

Laura and Elizabeth were out in the woods collecting whatever they could find to eat. Laura kept feeling like they were being watched.

"I want to go back to the camp," she told Elizabeth.

"Why? What's wrong?" asked Elizabeth.

"I'm not comfortable out here, I feel like somebody is watching us."

"You're just upset from what happened last night. We'll be fine."

Laura calmed down and they finished gathering food. When they arrived back at the campsite, Charles had a fire going and a primitive shelter built.

"This will have to do for now," he said.

"Looks fine," said Elizabeth.

"We have enough supplies for a few days," said Laura.

"This isn't a very productive area," Elizabeth added.

Charles replied, "Hopefully we are only here for a day or two before Sarah returns. Otherwise we wait until the full moon."

Laura wasn't comfortable with staying in the same place for longer than a day or two. She was worried that Brian may return. Even if Charles had been drunk the night before, Brian had just as much to drink. Charles obviously was no match for him.

"Just a couple days, then we look for a creek or a river to follow. That should lead us to a village," Elizabeth said.

Sarah was hot on her own trail from the night before. Then, from somewhere, she heard a cry of "Wolf!"

The sound of gunshots echoed through the air. Sarah dodged the bullets, but she had to leave her trail to find cover. She went down the nearest hole she could find. She was trying to catch her breath when she realized it had begun to rain. She was hoping it would only be a light rain, so she could stay on her trail, but it was anything but light. Sarah had to retreat out of her hole and take cover under some underbrush. Fortunately, the hunters had moved on.

Elizabeth, Charles, and Laura took cover under the shelter Charles had made. They were huddled together to avoid being dripped on. The rain had extinguished the fire. Suddenly they heard some rustling in the brush.

"Sarah!" Charles shouted.

There was no reply. Just as Charles was going to shout again, three men came out of the brush. The men noticed Charles and the girls right away.

"What are you doing out here?" one of the men asked.

The girls huddled behind Charles and let him do all the talking.

"We're heading toward a village not too far from here," he said.

"We're heading to the village ourselves" the man replied, "and we have a wagon not too far from here. You probably don't want stay here without protection. We just shot a wolf pretty close to here."

"Just wait a minute," replied Charles. He turned to the girls to get their input.

"Maybe it's the village we've been looking for," he said.

"I'm cold and miserable," replied Laura. "Let's go."

"You two go," Elizabeth said. "I'll wait here for Sarah."

"You heard them say they just shot a wolf. She's not coming back," said Charles.

"I've made up my mind. I'll wait here for a couple of days for Sarah. If we haven't showed up in the village by then, come back and get me," said Elizabeth.

Charles and Laura said their goodbyes to Elizabeth and headed out with the hunters. Elizabeth stepped out to try to relight the fire.

"By the way, my name is Charles, and this is Laura," Charles said to the hunter.

"My name is Jesse," the hunter said, "and these are my boys Zachary and Ezekiel. You can call them Zach and Zeke. When we get home, I'll have Molly fix you both up a hot bath. Laura, you look about her size, so you should be able to wear some of her clothes."

"Thanks," said Laura.

"If you don't mind me asking, what happened?" asked Jesse.

"We don't want to discuss it right now," replied Charles.

As they rounded the bend, they could see the wagon.

A smile appeared on Laura's face as Zeke helped her up into it.

Sarah came out from the underbrush, shook herself dry, and tried to relocate her scent. With all the rain it was no use, and in all the commotion she had lost her sense of direction. She wandered around, trying to find any of her scent. She was about to give up when she smelled something burning. She followed that scent.

Laura, Charles, and the hunters arrived at the village just as the sun was setting. Jesse introduced them to his wife Molly, and she got them some hot bath water going. Laura insisted that Molly stay with her while she bathed.

"Honey, why are you so nervous?" Molly asked.

"I was raped," replied Laura.

"By who? It wasn't one of my boys, was it?"

"No! The man who raped me was supposed to help us find a village. He assaulted me and left us where your husband and sons found us. My friend Elizabeth is still there, waiting for another of our friends. Sarah, Elizabeth, and I had an argument, and Sarah took off. Elizabeth is alone out there and I fear that Brian will come back and hurt her."

Molly cringed. "Well, you'll be safe here," she said.

Laura finished her bath and Molly gave her some clothes to wear. Just as Jesse thought, Laura and Molly were nearly the same size. Laura and Molly went to the kitchen and Laura helped make supper.

When Charles finished with his bath, he went to find Jesse and his sons. He volunteered to help with the chores before supper. He wasn't used to tending to livestock, but he helped Zach and Zeke milk the cows and feed the horses.

Sarah followed the smell of the smoke. She changed back into human form before leaving the woods to enter the tiny village. She walked around the village and saw that it seemed to be abandoned. The smoke she had smelled was from one of the houses that had burnt and was still smoldering.

It was getting dark, so she decided to take shelter in one of the houses. She walked into the house, which looked inside as though someone had left in a hurry. There was food, wood for a fire, and a bed. She made a fire in the fireplace, cooked some food, and then turned in for the night.

Laura and Charles ate supper with Jesse and his family. Laura helped Molly clean up afterward. Molly then showed Laura where she would be sleeping.

"This is my daughter's room. You can sleep in here."

"Daughter's room? You never mentioned anything about having a daughter," said Laura.

"We had a daughter," replied Molly.

"What do you mean, had a daughter?"

"Her name was Nellie. She went to gather berries one morning and never came back. The whole village searched for her, but her body was never found."

"Did she have any reason to take off?"

"Well, she was in love with a man that Jesse and I didn't approve of."

"Why didn't you approve of him?"

"He was a drifter. He just showed up in the village one day, asking if anything needed painting. My Nellie fell for him fast. Before we knew it, he was asking our permission to marry her. I didn't even know his name when he asked us. Now I can't stand to say his name or even hear it."

Laura looked Molly right in the eyes. "You don't need to say his name. I know what it is, because when I said who assaulted me, I saw you," said Laura. She hugged Molly.

Sarah had settled into one of the abandoned houses in the village. She rummaged through what was left in the house. She found some more food and a change of clothes. She nibbled on some of the food, and by the light of the fire, she wrote in her diary.

April 26, 1895: I've been away from the others for a few days now. I hope everything is fine with them. I stumbled upon a village today that was recently abandoned. Luckily, I found a house that isn't in bad of shape and is fully stocked. I'll snoop around in the morning. Hopefully this is the village Brian was talking about and the others will be here in the morning. I feel terrible for leaving the others. I just wish they felt as strongly as I do about this mission. I hope I don't fail Benjamin.

Sarah cuddled up with some blankets and fell asleep.

Elizabeth was getting paranoid being by herself. Every noise she heard scared her. She thought it was Brian coming back to finish his business.

"Only one more night until the full moon," she said to herself.

She snuggled in front of the fire and turned in for the night.

"The full moon starts in two days," Charles said.

"I know," Laura replied. "What are we going to do?"

"We need to explore the village tomorrow," said Charles.

"Molly told me something tonight that is very interesting."

"What?" asked Charles.

"Molly and Jesse had a daughter named Nellie. She fell for a man who appeared in town looking to do some painting. Obviously, it was Brian. It wasn't long before he asked permission for marriage. Molly and Jesse didn't approve of him or trust him, since they barely knew him. Nellie went off picking berries one morning and never came back. A body was never found."

"Before Brian assaulted you, I wouldn't have believed it. But now I wouldn't put anything past him."

Laura responded, "I believe we're in the right village. But I also believe that Brian lied to us. I think he was leading us into a trap. Knowing that Elizabeth is out there on her own weighs on my mind."

"I'll talk to Jesse in the morning about going and getting her," said Charles.

During the night, Elizabeth was awakened by a loud sound. A howl echoed through the air.

She jumped up, expecting to see Sarah. But Sarah wasn't what she saw. Instead, she saw exactly the creature Brian had described. She took off running and screaming. The animal gave chase. Elizabeth ran as fast as she could, but the animal was gaining. She was becoming short of breath, so she decided to climb the nearest tree. She climbed as high as she could and held on tight. The animal shook the tree, but the trunk was too thick to shake aggressively.

"Help! Help!" Elizabeth yelled as loud as she could.

Sarah was tossing and turning when she heard the screams. She went outside to investigate.

"Help!" echoed through the air again.

Sarah changed into a wolf and followed the screams. She put her nose to the air and sniffed. The closer she got to the screams, the more cautious she became. She knew that she would be no competition for what she had smelled.

She unfortunately had to lay back, wait, and hope her scent didn't carry. She found a brush pile and hid under it. The bloodcurdling screams raised her adrenaline level, but she knew she needed to remain calm and stay away from any altercations.

A few hours passed and the screaming finally stopped. Sarah looked out from under the brush pile and noticed that the sun was coming up. She figured that what she smelled would be gone by now, fearing that it would be seen by humans. She changed back into human form and went to investigate. She didn't have to go far to smell the territory the animal had marked. She looked up into the tree.

"Looks like it treed a raccoon," she shouted up the tree.

"Sarah! Is that really you?" Elizabeth shouted down.

"Yes, it's me. Where are the others?"

"Let me get down and then I'll explain."

Elizabeth climbed down the tree, ran over to Sarah, and gave her a big hug.

"Where are the others?" Sarah asked again. "It's a full moon tomorrow night."

Elizabeth replied, "They left with some hunters yesterday."

"They did what?"

"Let's get back to the campsite and I'll tell you everything."

Chapter 14

Charles awakened to the sound of Zeke and Zach milking cows. He got up and went to help.

"You are a guest. You really don't need to help," said Zach.

"I want to help," Charles replied. "And I need a favor."

"What's that?" asked Zeke.

"We need to go back and get Elizabeth this morning."

"Shouldn't be a problem once we are done with the chores," replied Zeke.

Elizabeth and Sarah sat on a log as Elizabeth filled Sarah in on what had happened. When the tale was told, Sarah looked down.

"I'm so sorry," she said finally. "We need to find them."

Elizabeth pointed in the direction the hunters had led Laura and Charles. Then she asked, "What was that thing that chased me up the tree? It looked like what Brian described to us."

"That's what it was: a lycan," answered Sarah.

The two of them headed off in search of their friends.

Charles, Zach, and Zeke finished all their chores, and Zach went to talk to Jesse.

"Dad, can Zeke and I take Charles back to get his other lady friend?"

"Not right now, Zach. Your mother and I have to runs some eggs and things to Mrs. Esserman," Jesse answered.

Zach went back to the barn to let Charles and Zeke know they couldn't use the wagon right away.

Sarah and Elizabeth had been wandering around for hours with no signs of a village or even any houses.

"Let's go back," said Sarah.

"I don't want to go back there for another night," replied Elizabeth.

"We can get back to the village I stayed in last night. Tomorrow begins the full moon and we will be able to cover more ground at night."

The two of them headed back toward the village.

Zeke, Zach, Charles, and Laura were waiting on Jesse and Molly to return from Mrs. Esserman's house.

"They should have been here hours ago," said Zeke.

Zach replied, "Knowing Mom and Dad they just lost track of time talking."

"We only have a few hours of daylight," Charles said. "We need to go get our friend."

"We can't get there and back on foot by nightfall," replied Zach.

"I'm not going to let her stay out there another night by herself," responded Charles.

"I would advise you not to go out in the woods after dark, Charles," said Zach.

Charles ignored Zach. He and Laura headed out to find the campsite.

About an hour had passed when Jesse and Molly arrived back home.

"Where are our guests?" asked Molly.

Zach answered, "They headed back to their campsite to get their friend."

"How long ago did they leave?" asked Jesse.

"About an hour ago," replied Zach.

"Boys, hop in the wagon, Molly, you get into the house. We need to find them as soon as possible!" shouted Jesse.

Elizabeth and Sarah were making good time back to the village. Sarah looked at the sun.

"We have about 45 minutes of light left. We should be there before dark," she said.

"Do we need to gather anything?"

"No, everything that we need is there. The house looks as if someone left in a hurry."

Charles and Laura were almost halfway to the campsite when Charles tripped over some vines. He fell to the ground and immediately grabbed his ankle.

"Damn! I think I broke it!" shouted Charles.

Laura knelt down beside Charles. "Let me see it," she said.

Laura assisted Charles in removing his boot and sock. She looked at his ankle.

"Ouch!" she said.

"Stop being sarcastic. It really hurts!" shouted Charles.

"I wasn't being sarcastic. I know it hurts. There's a bone sticking out."

Laura left Charles on the ground for a little while as she searched for something to make a splint from. She found a few fallen branches that would work. She headed back to Charles with them. She tore a few strips of cloth off her dress and began to splint Charles's ankle.

"How does it feel? It's not too tight, is it?" she asked.

"It feels better, but we need to find some shelter. Night will be upon us soon."

Laura helped Charles up. He put his arm around her to keep the weight off his ankle. They hobbled into the woods and found a cave. Charles sat down on a stump as Laura went into the cave to make sure it would be suitable. She soon returned.

"It should be fine. It's pretty deep, so we should be able to stay out of the elements."

It was getting too dark to gather wood or anything to eat. The two of them crawled deep into the cave and huddled close together to keep warm.

Jesse and the boys searched until dark. They returned home to let Molly know that they didn't find them.

"We must pray for their safety," she said.

The four of them knelt down and began to pray.

"To he who controls the night, bring our friends what they deserve. Sacrifice their flesh for the good of our breed," they prayed.

They got off their knees and Jesse pointed at the boys.

"Go find them, boys!" he shouted.

Zach and Zeke went off after them.

Sarah and Elizabeth arrived at the village and settled in.

"I'm going out for a little bit," Sarah said.

"Why?" asked Elizabeth.

"I need to make sure that the lycan doesn't come back around."

Sarah changed into wolf form and headed out. Elizabeth settled in for the night.

Laura and Charles were asleep deep in the cave. Laura was awoken by some noise at the mouth of the cave.

"I think someone is here," she whispered to Charles.

"Just be quiet," he replied sleepily. "No one will be looking for us until morning."

Laura and Charles lay motionless on the ground. Soon the noise was gone and the two of them fell back asleep.

Laura could see the morning light peeking through the mouth of the cave. She nudged Charles to wake him up. She helped him make it to the entrance of the cave and out into the sun. Charles sat on a stump as Laura tended to his ankle.

"We need to find you help before nightfall," she said.

Charles replied, "I know, but I'm only going to slow you down. You head back and find Jesse and his family."

Laura helped Charles back into the cave and gathered him some food and water. Then she headed back toward the village.

Zach and Zeke returned home empty-handed. Jesse met them at the door.

"Well, boys?" he said.

They lowered their heads. "We couldn't find them," answered Zach.

Jesse took the boys to the barn. He grabbed the horsewhip and began to whip the boys. "You boys failed him!" shouted Jesse.

He continued to beat them until they bled. The boys fell to their knees and begged Jesse for mercy.

"Don't beg for pity from me, boys. You need to appease him," he said.

Just then, a man came out of a stall.

"You're pathetic!" he shouted at the boys.

"We're sorry, master. Give us one more chance and we will find them."

"It's too late. Tonight they will travel and we'll have to follow them," the man replied.

"Then we should get them now," said Zeke.

"Patience, my boy," said Jesse.

The man went back into the stall and Jesse took the boys into the house so Molly could tend to their wounds. Molly met them at the door.

"Why do you boys make your father do this to you?" she shouted.

The boys lowered their heads again. Not a word was muttered. Molly began to bandage them up.

"You two are beginning to disgrace our family. This doesn't bode well for us."

Sarah and Elizabeth made their way back to the old campsite. Sarah sniffed around in the air, finally finding a scent. She led Elizabeth into the woods. Elizabeth struggled to keep up with her.

Laura was trying to find her way back to Jesse and Molly's village. She wasn't too confident in her sense of direction, though. She soon realized she was going around in circles. She was so frustrated that she decided to sit down on a stump and try to collect her thoughts.

Molly sat with Jesse on the front porch.

"Where did we go wrong raising our children?" she asked.

Jesse answered, "They don't have to suffer the consequences we did growing up. Sure, I whipped them, but by tonight they will be healed. They need to suffer just like Nellie did."

Jesse went into the house and hollered for the boys. "Zach! Zeke! Get down here!"

Zach and Zeke came down the ladder from their room. They went outside with Jesse.

"Boys, I'm going to give you one more chance. Don't let us down. I'm tired of having to explain your ignorance," Jesse demanded.

"We won't let you down, Father." They headed out to search for Laura and Charles.

Laura still couldn't get her sense of direction. She was sitting on a stump with her face in her hand and bent over in frustration. She felt something cold on the top of her head. She peeked through her hands and what she saw startled her. When she got up and began to run, she tripped over some brush and was knocked out cold.

Zach and Zeke were out searching for Laura and Charles.

"Let's go back to that cave," said Zeke.

"We can't be messing around, Zeke," said Zach.

"Come on, Zach, let's go," whined Zeke.

Before Zach could say another word, Zeke was off and running toward the cave. Zach gave chase.

Sarah had lost the trail she was following. Now she and Elizabeth found themselves in the middle of the woods, surrounded by trees. Sarah turned back into human form and the two of the sat on a log to talk.

"We should rest. It's going to be dark soon and we will be able to cover more ground," Sarah said.

"I really think we should search more while we still have light," replied Elizabeth.

Sarah had been awake most of the night and was

exhausted, but she went along with Elizabeth. They continued to search.

Laura was waking up; she was very groggy. Through her heavy eyes she could make out the interior of a barn. Laura shook the cobwebs out of her head. She tried to get up, and that's when she discovered she was shackled to the wall.

"Help!" she yelled.

Standing in front of the light through the door, so she couldn't see anything except his silhouette, was a man.

"Don't worry, my pet," he said. "You won't be harmed."

"What do you want with me?" shouted Laura.

"I don't want you. I want what's inside you," he replied.

The man came up to Laura, forced her to drink a liquid, and left.

Zach and Zeke approached the mouth of the cave and went inside. Zach took a big whiff of the air.

"Smell that, Zeke?"

Zeke inhaled deeply. "I sure do, Zach," he replied.

They continued deeper into the cave, where they found Charles lying on the ground.

"What are you doing in here, Charles?" asked Zeke.

Charles replied, "I broke my ankle. I sent Laura to find you guys. I guess she did."

"We haven't seen Laura," Zach replied.

"How did you know I was here, then?" asked Charles.

"Don't worry about that. We need to get back to the house before it gets dark," replied Zach.

Charles then remembered that it was a full moon that night.

"No, just leave me here in the cave until Laura comes back for me. Just come back in the morning to get us," he said.

Zach replied in a very deep voice, "You'll come with us now if you know what's good for you."

Charles was getting ready to say something when he noticed Zach's eyes glowing red. "Okay, I'll go," he said.

Zach and Zeke helped Charles up. "We'd thought you see it our way," said Zach.

Elizabeth and Sarah continued to search. They came upon a cave and Sarah sniffed the air.

"Charles and Laura were here, but so was somebody else," she said. "We'll wait here until dark."

Zach and Zeke arrived back at their house with Charles.

"Father!" shouted Zeke.

Jesse came out of the house. Zach and Zeke laid Charles at his feet.

"Good job, boys," Jesse said. "Let's get him into the barn."

Zach picked Charles up and carried him into the barn. Jesse ordered that Charles be put into a stall.

Zach laughed. "Only a few more minutes," he said.

"What are you talking about?" asked Charles.

"You'll see, our pet," replied Zach.

Before Charles could utter another word, he discovered what Zach was talking about. He began to change into a wolf. Charles was helpless with the broken ankle, but changing into a wolf would help him heal faster. As Charles lay in the stall, beginning to heal, Zach and Zeke begin throwing rocks at him.

"Here, boy, come get it," laughed Zeke.

"Fetch, boy," laughed Zach.

They had fun with Charles for a while before Charles finally had enough. He tried to put some weight on his hind leg and jump out of the stall. He wasn't able to put enough pressure on his leg to make the jump. Zach started to climb into the stall. Charles growled at him.

"Come on!" shouted Zach.

Charles raised the hair on his back, showed his teeth, and began to growl more aggressively. Zach took Jesse's whip and began whipping Charles. This caused Charles to lunge at Zach.

Charles then felt something around his throat. Zach had caught him in mid-air by the throat. Zach had begun to change. Zach went through his transformation and became a lycan. He threw Charles up against the wall of the stall. Charles fought as hard as he could, but in the midst of the battle Zach was able to grab him again by the throat. He let out a bloodcurdling howl and ripped Charles's trachea from his throat. He threw the limp body to the ground.

Zeke and Jesse then transformed into lycans as well. The three of them threw their heads into the air and loosed their victory howls.

Elizabeth and Sarah heard the howls of the lycans. They stopped in their tracks, knowing they would be no match for the lycans if they were to run into them. Sarah turned to Elizabeth and motioned her in a different direction.

Chapter 15

When Laura awoke she was still in the barn, but she was confused. She knew it was supposed to be the night of the full moon, but she hadn't changed. She wondered if whatever the man had given her to drink had kept her from changing. She began to scream.

Laura's screams reached Sarah and Elizabeth, so they followed the sound. They traveled for about 45 minutes when they cautiously came up to a barn. They could hear Laura inside. Sarah took a big sniff of the air, and what she smelled was all too familiar to her. She again motioned with her head to Elizabeth and the two of them retreated into the woods to take cover until morning.

Dawn had come and Jesse and the boys had returned to the house. Jesse instructed the boys to do their chores. He returned to the barn and looked at Charles's body.

"What a waste," he said.

Jesse then went to tend to his own chores. He didn't get too far before he called for Zack and Zeke to come to him.

"Boys, we need to get rid of any evidence of what took place here last night. We don't want anyone to think there are wolves in these parts," he said.

Zach and Zeke picked up the wolf carcass and took it to the burn pile. They stood by the fire celebrating while it burned.

Sarah and Elizabeth crawled out of their shelter.

"We need to go back and get her," said Elizabeth.

"We can't get her," replied Sarah.

"Why not?" asked Elizabeth.

"I can't tell you. We need to get back to Benjamin. He might be the only one who can do anything about it."

"Can't we see if she is all right?"

"No, we need to get far away from here as fast as we can. Brian has led us into a trap. I can't believe I was so stupid and fell for it."

"What do you mean, a trap?" asked Elizabeth.

"Don't you get it? Couldn't you smell it last night? We are surrounded by lycans. Brian knew what we are. That is what made him change his mind. He wanted me but he settled for Laura. He is going to use her to start his own pack. Laura is pregnant from being raped."

"So what do we do now?" asked Elizabeth.

"Just get back to Benjamin as soon as possible," answered Sarah.

Sarah then looked at Elizabeth. She looked her right in the eye. "I have something planned for you," she said.

"What?" asked Elizabeth.

"You'll know what to do when it presents itself. For now, we need to find water and follow it."

Eventually they found a river and were trying to find a place to get some rest. It was late afternoon and the two of them sat in silence, not knowing what would happen to them in the next few days. Finally, the silence was broken.

"I'm scared," said Elizabeth.

"I am too, Elizabeth," replied Sarah. "I'm so sorry that I got you into this whole situation. I should have been able to see through Brian, but he was able to block his thoughts from me."

"I knew it was too good to be true," said Elizabeth. "I feel bad for Benjamin and everything that happened to him when he was younger, but is all this worth it? There were four of us when this adventure started and now there may be only two of us. I know he saved our village, but I think his obsession with this Ryan is going to be the downfall of all of us. I just want to get home."

"Don't blame Benjamin. I am to blame also. I've been jealous of Ellen ever since Benjamin fell for her. I've been trying to do everything that I could to get him to really notice me, so I keep the idea that we can save his sister alive so I have my chance to impress him and steal him away from Ellen. I've taken my obsession too far, and if I'm correct about Brian, I don't deserve anybody. I deserve to be alone."

"I had no idea you had feelings for Benjamin. I've always looked at you two like a brother and sister."

"Well, at any rate, we really need to get going," Sarah said. "We have something to find before it gets dark."

Laura was still in the barn. She was confused. The man who had given her the liquid the other night hadn't returned. Instead, a young girl brought her food and water. The girl had already been in twice today, and had even helped Laura clean up. Laura could tell by the light coming through the cracks in the barn that there wasn't much sunlight left in the day.

She heard the door open. She was still expecting the man, but it was the young girl again with food and water. The girl unlatched one of the arm shackles as she had done before so Laura could eat and drink. The girl then did the unexpected: she unshackled Laura's legs. Laura was thankful. She began stretching her legs.

"You mustn't tell," said the girl.

"I won't," Laura promised.

Laura ate her food and drank her water. Before the girl left, she re-shackled Laura. It was now dark and again Laura didn't change. She was again confused because the man hadn't brought her anything. Then she realized he must know she would trust the little girl. In all likelihood the liquid was in the food and water the girl brought. Laura sat miserably until she fell asleep.

Elizabeth and Sarah had just entered a small barnyard, just off from the river. They ran into a young man on the farm. They tried to get him to come with them into the woods, but he wouldn't.

"Witches!" he yelled as he ran to the house.

Moments later, the farmer was back out with his shotgun. "Stay off my property, witches!" he shouted.

In all the commotion, the farmer forgot about his young daughter coming back from gathering. Sarah went over and grabbed her. The young girl screamed.

The farmer shouted, "Nora!"

He ran off the porch toward Sarah and Elizabeth. Sarah scratched the girl to get her to bleed.

"Finish her!" she shouted at Elizabeth.

Elizabeth stared at her. "I can't!" she shouted.

"Do it now!" demanded Sarah.

Elizabeth's fangs grew; she bit the girl on the throat. The warm blood filled her mouth, and her eyes rolled to the back of her head. She dropped the girl and instantly changed into a wolf. Sarah did the same, and they were off and running. The farmer ran up to find his daughter's lifeless body. He fired a few rounds out of his shotgun, but he didn't hit what he was aiming for.

Sarah and Elizabeth were now able to stay in wolf form, and headed back toward their home village.

It was the last night of the full moon. Laura still hadn't seen the man since the first night she was in the barn. She had refused to drink any water or eat any food for the last few days, convinced that the man kept her from changing by putting something into her food and water. Nevertheless, she still hadn't changed all week. She was weak and hungry. Dusk was approaching, and her stomach was cramping from hunger and dehydration. The young girl had brought food and water, but Laura again refused it.

"You need to eat," said the young girl.

"I'd rather die," said Laura.

The young girl again unshackled Laura. "Remember, you mustn't tell," she said.

Laura looked at the girl. "Why are you being so nice to me?" she asked.

"Because he told me to," the girl said.

"Who told you to?"

The girl pointed. "He did," she said.

Laura looked where the girl was pointing, and there the man stood. He looked outside. "Any time now," he said.

He walked up to the girl and Laura. It was too dark in the barn for Laura to make out his face.

Suddenly Laura began to change. The little girl screamed. When the change was complete, she was still weak from dehydration and starvation.

"Go ahead," the man said. "You know you want to."

He hit the little girl on the side of the head with a pitchfork. The girl fell to the ground and her wound began to bleed. Even with her hunger, she fought the urge to eat the little girl as hard as she could. But something was taking over her human emotions. She struggled with the urges, but the hunger touched her animal instincts, and she tore into the little girl. The whole time Laura was feasting, the man laughed.

"You are no longer my pet," he said. "You're now my mate."

He changed into a lycan, and the two of them headed off into the woods.

Chapter 16

It had been several weeks since Sarah and the others had left on their quest to find Ryan and my sister. The mood in the village was good; Ellen had recently told me she was pregnant again.

The week of the full moon ended and almost all of the planting was done. We were out collecting wood when we noticed two familiar faces coming up the path. I ran out to meet them; it was Sarah and Elizabeth. They both looked exhausted, so instead of drilling them with questions we decided to let them rest. I stayed out into late evening waiting for Charles and Laura to return, but they didn't. Keeping Jason away from Sarah drove Ellen insane. She finally got him to bed and came out to get me.

"Let's get some rest, Benjamin," she told me. I refused at first, but I knew that she was getting frustrated, so I gave in and went to bed.

I awoke early in the morning, eager to talk to Sarah, but all she wanted to do was spend time with Jason.

"Boy, you've grown. I missed you so much," she kept telling him.

I could tell from her voice and her actions that

something was wrong. I also knew that she would only talk when she was ready.

Eventually it was time for Jason to go to bed. Sarah helped Ellen tuck him in and then smothered him with kisses. I went out on the front porch and sat in my rocker. I had just started whittling on some wood when the door opened. It was Ellen.

"I'm worried about Sarah," she said as she sat next to me.

"I am too," I replied.

"I know she hasn't seen Jason in a few months, but she has never acted like this with him before."

"Something must have happened while she was gone. I need to talk to her."

"Give her tonight to rest. We'll see how she is in the morning, then we'll talk to her."

I awoke to the sound of a knocking at the door. I was greeted there by Elizabeth's mother, Josephine.

"She's gone! She's gone!" she screamed.

"Josephine, calm down. What's wrong?" I asked.

"Elizabeth is gone. Something must have happened while they were gone, Benjamin. But I couldn't get her to talk to me about anything."

"I'll get some answers from Sarah. Let's wait and see if Elizabeth comes back."

I walked Josephine back to her house and made her some coffee. I sat with her until I felt comfortable enough to leave her by herself.

Ellen was waiting for me in the kitchen as I walked through the back door.

"What's going on?" she asked.

"Elizabeth took off last night. I need to get answers from Sarah. I just have a bad feeling," I said.

Ellen replied, "I'll take Jason over to Mom and Dad's so Sarah isn't preoccupied with him."

"You mean more like using him as an excuse not to talk," I said.

"That's exactly what I mean."

Ellen began to make breakfast. I went out on the porch to finish my coffee and relax.

When about an hour had passed, Sarah joined me on the porch.

"Ellen already told me about Elizabeth. I should probably tell you what happened," she said.

"Probably. Josephine is very upset."

Sarah sighed, then told me everything that had happened since she had left with Laura, Elizabeth, and Charles. Her tale took some time. When she was finished, I was very disappointed.

"You were supposed to keep everyone together," I said.

"I'm sorry, Benjamin," she said.

I was floored by all the information, but now I understood why Elizabeth was unable to sleep. Not knowing what happened to my friends saddened me. Sarah only assumed that they had been killed; she didn't know for sure. She looked at me.

"Benjamin, they're gone. Trust me. Don't risk it," she said.

I paused, then spoke.

"Sarah I'm sorry you had to go through all that. My desire to find my sister has grown out of control, and now some of my friends have been hurt. Even though you disobeyed my orders, I will not punish you. As far as I'm concerned, not a word of what happened on your journey is to be spoken about. If anyone asks about them, they chose to live somewhere else."

"What about Elizabeth?" asked Sarah.

"I'll deal with Elizabeth when she comes back," I said.

Sarah gave me a hug. "Thank you," she said as she went back into the house.

A few hours passed. I saw Ellen and Jason walking through the barnyard. I waited for them to come up to the porch. I grabbed Jason and gave him a big hug. "I love you, buddy," I said to him.

I motioned for Ellen to come to me.

"What do you need?" she asked.

"Take Jason in. We need to talk."

She took Jason in the house to play with Sarah. Then she came back out on the porch.

"Did you talk with Sarah?" she asked.

"Yes, I did, and now I understand why Elizabeth is having trouble sleeping. I've had a bad feeling about the whole thing. Sarah confirmed my feelings."

"What happened?" asked Ellen.

"I'll tell you later. Right now I need to see if I can find Elizabeth."

I went to the edge of the barnyard to change into a wolf. I then went searching for Elizabeth.

Ellen went into the house and found Sarah and Jason playing. She sat in the chair and watched for a while. Jason began becoming cranky, so Ellen put him down. She came out of Jason's room and was met by Sarah.

"Where's Benjamin?" she asked.

"He went after Elizabeth," replied Ellen.

"How long has he been gone?"

"About an hour," Ellen replied.

Sarah started to leave, but Ellen stopped her. "We need to talk."

The two of them went into the kitchen and sat down.

"What happened while you were gone?" asked Ellen.

Sarah replied, "I don't really want to discuss it with you."

"Why not?"

"Because in your condition you don't need to know what we went through. I would never be able to live with myself if something happened to you or the baby."

"My condition? I'm only pregnant! Why won't you tell me?" Ellen shouted.

The commotion woke Jason up. The girls set aside their conversation and tended to him.

I followed Elizabeth's trail well away from the village. After a few hours, I decided to head back home and try to get some more information out of Sarah. When I arrived, I saw Ellen sitting alone on a bench in the park. I went into the park and approached her.

"What are you doing here?" I asked her.

"It's Sarah," she replied.

"What about Sarah?"

"I asked her what was going on and she threw 'my condition' in my face."

"I'll have a talk with her and fill you in later," I told her.

"Tell me later? Benjamin, you've been telling me that as long as I've known you. Yes, you gave me powers to survive the bee sting, and then you saved the village. But all we know is that we change when it's a full moon. Why can you and Sarah change whenever you want?"

I just told her, "I need to speak to Sarah, and I'll talk to you later."

Sarah and Jason were on the floor playing when I walked through the door. Luckily, Ellen wasn't far behind me. She took over occupying Jason while Sarah and I went out on the porch.

"Sarah, I tracked Elizabeth's trail for a few hours today, and I think she is heading back to where you came from," I said.

"I knew it!" she replied. "She didn't want to leave them there, but like I said, they aren't alive."

"I know, but what should we do? Should we follow her?" I asked.

"No, Benjamin. It's too dangerous!" shouted Sarah.

Ellen came to the door just as Sarah finished. "What's too dangerous?" she asked.

I sighed. "Okay, Ellen, sit down. It's time that we have that talk."

She sat down on the steps, and Sarah and I began to explain what was going on.

"So," Sarah said as she was winding down the tale, "we tracked Laura and Charles, but every lead had lycan scent all around. Laura and Charles are probably dead."

"Oh!" shouted Ellen.

"We don't know that for sure," I added.

"Oh, it had nothing to do with that," Ellen said, laughing a little. "The baby just kicked."

"Anyway, that's what's going on," Sarah said. "I told Benjamin that it's too dangerous to go after Elizabeth if she went back after Laura and Charles."

Ellen said, "I think there has been too much adventure around here lately. The new baby will be here in a few months, so you need to direct your attention to your family and the village."

"I know, Ellen," I answered.

I got up to leave.

"Benjamin, where do you think you're going?" shouted Ellen.

"I was going out to check with Mike at the mill," I replied.

"You still have some explaining to do," she said.

I headed back into the kitchen and sat down at the table. Jason came into the kitchen; he had just awoken from his nap. Sarah walked through the door, scooped him up, and took him into the family room to play. Ellen waited until Sarah and Jason were in the family room, then she looked at me.

"What else do you have to tell me?" asked Ellen.

I knew the time had finally come to explain what she was and why Sarah and I were different from her.

"Sarah, Elizabeth, and I are different from you because we have tasted human flesh," I explained.

She looked at me for a moment. "You're a monster," she whispered.

"You know I'm no monster. I only did it to protect us from Ryan."

"Protect us from Ryan? Why would he come back after you, Benjamin?"

"Not after me. He would be after Sarah," I told her.

"Why Sarah?" she asked.

"Sarah came from Ryan's village. I met her in my quest to find Ashley. Ryan was gone on a hunting trip at the time. He returned to the village early, and Sarah and I left so Ryan wouldn't know that I was there."

"So what makes you different from him?"

"Since I tasted human flesh, I have the ability to change at will. But I still have all my human emotions that work with my canine senses. I don't have any urge to attack humans or eat human flesh. If I did, I would be a lycan. I would lose all control, and then I would be a monster."

"What was it like?" Ellen asked me. "What was it like when you tasted human flesh? What was the person like?"

"The taste of the flesh and the blood flowing into my mouth was exhilarating. The man I killed was a drunk who was abusive to his family. He deserved to die," I said.

Ellen looked away and stared at the floor for a moment. I was just getting ready to get up from the table.

"Change me!" she shouted finally. "I want to have the same abilities as you and Sarah. Then you won't have to leave me out of things, and Sarah won't treat me like I'm different."

"Not now," I replied.

"That's always your answer!" shouted Ellen. "When?" She stormed out the door and away from the house.

I gave her a few minutes to calm down, and then I went after her. I knew where she was heading. I went directly to the bench in the park, and there she was. I went over to the bench and sat down beside her.

"I can't change you now," I told her.

"Why not?"

"Because you're pregnant. I don't know if anything would happen to the baby or not."

She turned and looked me right in the eyes.

"As soon as the baby is old enough, I want you to change me," she said.

"I will," I said. "As soon as the baby is old enough."

We sat on the park bench for a while, enjoying the peace and quiet. It was beginning to get dark so we headed back toward the house. We got back to find that Sarah had already tucked Jason in for the night. The three of us sat down at the table.

"Ellen asked to be changed tonight," I said.

"We can't do that with her condition," Sarah replied.

"I know," Ellen said, "but Benjamin promised me as soon as the baby is old enough, he will help me change and be like you the two of you."

Sarah rolled her eyes and got up from her chair.

"Please excuse me," she said.

She went outside. Ellen and I discussed the arrival of the new baby as we waited for her to come back, but soon we turned in for the night.

Sarah had gone to the same park bench where Ellen and I had been earlier that evening. I found out during a later discussion with Sarah that she spent a lot of time there while the rest of us slept. She was pining for someone she knew she couldn't have. I heard her come back into the house in the wee hours of the morning. I got up out of bed to talk to her, but she didn't want to talk.

Chapter 17

The months went by and soon it came time to do the harvesting. Ellen was miserable with the hot weather and being pregnant. She was due anytime. We still hadn't heard from Elizabeth, but otherwise things were going fine until the night of the full moon. Ellen's father and some others were out hunting when they came upon some human hunters. According to Jethro, they stood back, but the hunters kept coming. Ellen's father confronted the hunters and was shot and killed. Now I had to break the news to Ellen.

It was late in the morning when Ellen finally awoke. She made her way to the kitchen for some water. I gave her time to wake up, and then I sat with her at the table.

"Ellen, we need to talk," I told her.

"Why, what happened?" she asked. "Did Elizabeth come back or something?"

"No. It's about your father," I said.

"What about my father?"

"He's dead," I said softly.

Ellen had a blank look in her eyes.

I continued, "He was shot by some humans during the

hunt last night. The population of this area is growing so much, making our village more and more un-secluded. We will have to learn how to interact with humans invading our territory to keep this from happening again.

I don't think Ellen heard anything I said after "he's dead," because she still had the same blank stare on her face. She was showing no emotion and this concerned me. Then she began to cry. I went over to her to comfort her. Sarah came into the kitchen with Jason, but she noticed Ellen crying and took Jason back into the family room. I comforted Ellen until she had cried so much that she wasn't able to cry anymore. She went and sat down in the chair in the family room. Jason crawled up on her lap and snuggled against her. Sarah came into the kitchen.

"So you told her," Sarah said.

"Yes," I replied. "I knew she would take it hard, but I wasn't ready for that. She wasn't that emotional when her mother died."

"It's the hormones," replied Sarah.

Before we could say another word, we heard Ellen shouting from the family room: "It's time!"

Sarah and I ran into the family room. Jason was on the floor and Ellen was in the chair, holding her back and breathing hard.

"We need to hurry!" shouted Sarah.

We picked Ellen up and took her into the bedroom. I gathered everything that we were going to need while Sarah was tending to Ellen. I came back just as the baby began to crown. Sarah had a relieved look on her face. I knew it wasn't because I was there with the stuff; it was because the baby would be delivered before the full moon. We had been giving Ellen wolfsbane to keep her from changing the whole week of the full moon. We had forgotten that day, though, with what else was happening.

Sarah and I delivered the baby with no problems, then gave Ellen her wolfsbane. I was a proud father; Ellen had blessed me with a little girl. We named her Ashley after my sister. We let Ashley feed while Ellen rested. I brought Jason into the room to show him his little sister. As soon as everything was under control, Sarah took off. I was too busy tending to Jason to even notice she was gone.

Later, as Ellen and baby Ashley were both asleep, I went in to check on Jason, who was just waking up. I watched him as he stretched his little body and yawned.

"Do you want to see your little sister?" I asked.

A big smile popped up on his face. "No, Daddy, let's play," he said.

That surprised me. I thought he would be ecstatic to go see his new sister, but him wanting me to play with him made me realize that I needed to take more time for my family. Jason and I went outside and we played until it was almost dark.

It was last night of the full moon and Jason would have to go with the older kids in the safety barn while the rest of us hunted. I checked on Ellen and the baby; they were fine. Ellen was in the middle of nursing Ashley. I dropped off Jason at the safety barn, then met with the other villagers at our meeting place.

As the full moon began to rise, I noticed that Sarah wasn't with us, but I didn't have the time to look for her before we began to change. I led the pack out on the hunting expedition as Ellen's father had done the night before.

The night of hunting went well. As dawn approached, we all changed back into human form and began taking care of the previous night's bounty. The full moon was gone for a month, but we still had a funeral to take care of and harvesting to do, and I still saw no sign of Sarah.

I stopped by the barn and picked up Jason. I carried

him home while he slept and put him in his bed. I checked on Ellen and Ashley and they were both asleep. I checked Sarah's room but she wasn't there. I went to bed.

I woke to the sound of Ashley crying. Ellen had gotten out of bed and was nursing her. I sat up and looked out the window and noticed that it was past noon. I hopped out of bed and got dressed, then went to Ellen's Uncle George's house to discuss the funeral services for her father.

"Is there any other family we should notify?" I asked.

He replied, "There is another brother, Lester, but neither one of us liked him. And Ellen would be uncomfortable around him."

"Why would she be uncomfortable around him?" I asked.

"It's a long story. You should ask her yourself."

I thought for a moment. "Invite him anyway," I said.

George gave me a strange look. "Whatever you say, Benjamin."

We made a few more arrangements for the funeral. We wanted to give Ellen a few days with the new baby before we buried her father. I thanked George for all his help and headed out to the fields.

On my way out to the fields, I thought I saw Sarah, but it turned out to be another girl from the village. I made it out to the fields and checked how ready the crops were for harvest. I figured we had a few days after the funeral before we needed to harvest. That relieved some of my stress, but I still wondered how I was going to manage my family without Sarah around.

I walked through the door of my house and it was like I walked into a war zone. Jason had toys everywhere and Ashley was crying. Ellen was about ready to pull her hair out.

"He is acting out for attention, Benjamin. I can't feed

Ashley and keep him occupied!" she shouted.

"I'm sorry," I replied. "I was with your Uncle George, planning your father's funeral. He brought up your Uncle Lester."

"He did what?" shouted Ellen. "Why would he do that to me?"

"He said you might react like this, but we can discuss it later." Jason was pulling on my pants leg for attention.

"Okay," replied Ellen as she took Ashley to nurse.

I took Jason into the family room and we made a game of picking up his toys. Then I took him outside with me as I took care of some chores. We had to go to Ellen's family's farm and tend to the hogs. As we did so, a devious plan came to mind. I filed the plan in the back of my head and finished the chores. It was just beginning to get dark as we headed home.

Unlike earlier, the house was completely silent when we walked in. Ashley was sound asleep in her cradle and Ellen was asleep in the rocker. Jason and I went out to the kitchen, where Ellen had rabbit stew over the fire. It was almost done, so I set the table. After about half an hour, I was getting ready to dish it up when Ellen walked through the kitchen door.

"How long have I been sleeping?" she asked.

"I don't know," I replied. "By the way the stew looked, I'd say an hour or so."

"How long have you two been home?"

"Half an hour or so," I said.

Ellen noticed the table was already set.

"Go ahead and sit down," I told her.

She sat down and I dished stew for the three of us. We had a nice, quiet supper together.

Ellen had just finished the rest of her corn bread when Ashley began crying, breaking the silence we had enjoyed.

Ellen got up from the table went and got Ashley to change her diaper. Then she sat in the rocker and began to nurse as I cleaned up the kitchen with some help from Jason.

I went outside to get some water to clean up Jason and get him ready for bed. I looked in the window and could see Ellen by the candlelight, nursing Ashley. It reminded me of the first time I saw her sitting on the bench in the park. I stayed there looking for moment, then went back inside.

I got Jason into bed, then went back into the kitchen and made some coffee. I had just finished my coffee when Ellen walked in. She sat down with me at the table.

"We need to talk," she said.

"Yes, we do," I replied.

"Are you inviting my Uncle Lester to my father's funeral?"

"He is your father's brother," I said.

"But you don't understand!"

"Your Uncle George told me."

"He did what?" shouted Ellen.

I told her "You need to be a little quieter. You don't want to wake the baby."

Ellen began to cry. She tried to talk, but the memories brought up combined with the hormones from just having a baby to put her into a prolonged crying spell. I comforted her for a while until she finally stopped crying.

"I'm sorry," she said.

"Don't worry about it," I replied.

Ellen took a deep breath. "What did Uncle George tell you?" she asked.

"He just told me you would be uncomfortable around Lester, and that I should ask you why," I said

"That's all you told you?"

"Yes," I answered.

"Well, I really don't care if he comes or not," Ellen said.

Just then, Ashley started to cry, and Ellen went to tend to her. I wanted to talk to her more about this, but I knew she wasn't ready to tell me why she was so upset. I decided I would talk to George about it later.

Chapter 18

When morning came, I forced myself out of bed when Jason came into our room. I took him downstairs and ate breakfast with him. Then it was off to the farm to tend to the hogs, and back to George's house to finalize the funeral plans.

I asked George, "So what did Lester do to Ellen?"

"She didn't tell you? Well, I figured she wouldn't, out of embarrassment. Since he is going to be here tomorrow, I should probably tell you."

He started to speak, then remembered that I had Jason with me. "It isn't something the boy should hear. I'll tell you later."

Jason and I headed home. I walked in the door and could instantly smell the lunch Ellen was fixing.

"I'm guessing it's been a good day," I said.

Ellen smiled at me. "Ashley has been an angel today," she said.

I smiled back at Ellen as I took Jason to wash him up before lunch. When we came back, Ellen already had the table set and lunch on it. We sat down and ate. During lunch, we talked.

"Has my uncle arrived yet?" asked Ellen.

"He'll arrive tomorrow morning," I answered.

"Where will he be staying?"

"At your parents' farm," I answered.

"Oh, really?" Ellen asked in a sinister voice.

"What do you have up your sleeve?"

"Nothing," she replied.

I knew she had something in mind, but our discussion was cut short by a screaming baby. Ellen went and attended to Ashley while I cleaned up lunch. Then Jason and I went into the family room and played while Ellen fed Ashley. We wanted to continue our discussion, but by the time Ellen was done tending to Ashley and I with Jason, it was time to turn in for the night.

In the morning, George and I headed to Ellen's parents' house to await Lester's arrival. We didn't have to wait long before we heard the horses in the distance. Soon, Lester was coming around the bend. He parked his wagon by the barn and pointed at me.

"Boy, tend to my horses," he said.

I gave him a wicked glare. Before I could say anything, George spoke. "You need to take care of your own horses, Lester. He is not a servant to you."

Lester stared George down, but finally tied his horses up to the barn and came back to George and myself.

"So, the stupid son of a bitch went and got himself shot. I always said he was the dumb one," Lester said, laughing.

George just shook his head in disgust, then introduced us. "This is Benjamin. He is Ellen's husband."

"Oh, so you're the one who got the used goods," laughed Lester.

"That's enough, Lester!" shouted George.

Lester was really rubbing me the wrong way. I so badly wanted to change and kill him myself, but then I would be no better than Ryan. So I controlled my temper. Lester let himself into the house. George and I decided to leave to go get ready for the funeral.

I walked into the door and Ellen instantly knew that something was bothering me.

"Well. I take it that my Uncle Lester arrived safely," she said.

"Yes, he did, and it took everything I had to keep from killing him," I replied.

"He does have that sort of personality."

Soon it was time to head to the cemetery for the funeral. George met us on the way.

"Where's Lester?" I asked.

"Oh, he is probably already there. He is trying to take control of everything around here, just like he always has. It was a bad idea to invite him," George replied.

We were coming up on the cemetery, and George's suspicions appeared to be true. Lester was up with the preacher, trying to tell him how he was supposed to perform the ceremony. George went up and removed Lester so the preacher could get started with the funeral.

Ellen had Ashley wrapped in some blankets when Lester came up to her.

"So, wench, you think you're upstanding enough to be a mother," he said to her.

Ellen just looked away and ignored him.

"I'm talking to you, wench," he said, raising his voice a little.

Ellen again ignored him. Agitated, Lester then said something that he would soon regret.

"You know that picture of your family? I looked at it all day, fantasizing about that time. You remember, don't you?"

I got back to Ellen just after Lester had finished what

he was saying. She sat on the other side of me, putting me between her and Lester during the ceremony.

When the service was over, Ellen turned to me. "Take Ashley and Jason back to the house with you," she said. "I want to go back to Dad's house and grab something before Lester gets back there."

"Do you want me to go with you?" I asked.

"No, just get the kids home. I'll be home shortly," she replied.

The kids and I headed to our house while Ellen went to her childhood home. As I left I looked back and noticed George and Lester still talking to the preacher.

Ellen went inside the house and was looking all around for the picture Lester had mentioned, but she wasn't able to find it. Lester had made himself at home and most of the things that had belonged to Ellen's parents were moved or disturbed in some fashion.

Ellen was sifting through piles, looking for the picture. She didn't realize how much time she had spent there. Suddenly she heard the front door open and close. She hid in a closet in the room she was in. Then she heard a voice.

"I'm glad that's over. I don't know how much longer I can stand to be around the backward folks in this village."

To her horror, the voice she heard was that of her Uncle Lester. Ellen stood in the closet, panicking. She knew she needed to get home to tend to Ashley, but how would she do it?

After a few moments, her mind began to wander back to the night of her twelfth birthday. There had been a wonderful party with friends and family. Several family members were staying, Lester included, making the house crowded. Ellen had asked if she and a friend could sleep in the barn. Her father said yes, so she and her friend made their beds in the hayloft.

A few hours later, the girls began hearing noises in the barn. The noises scared Ellen's friend so badly that she had run home, leaving Ellen by herself in the loft. Ellen tried to go to sleep but soon was awoken by a different noise. This time she could make out a figure heading toward her. She kept quiet and hid under her blanket, but she felt someone grab her blanket and rip it off of her.

She tried to scream, but her mouth was covered before she could. She punched and kicked, to no avail. Through the dim light peeking through the barn she could make out her Uncle Lester's face.

He said drunkenly "It's time to teach this family a lesson." So, you stupid wench, I'm going to have my way with you, and if you want to keep your family safe you won't tell anybody."

He grabbed Ellen by the shirt and began to violently shake her. Ellen was trying to fight back but her uncle was too strong for her to fight off. He kept shaking her until she lost consciousness. She didn't regain consciousness until the next morning, but something didn't seem right. She wondered what had happened, but mentioned nothing to her family for fear that her uncle would live up to his promise.

Ellen began to get angry. She needed to get home and he wasn't going to stop her, or hurt her again. She burst out of the closet and ran for the front door. Before she could make it, Lester cut her off.

"So, you liked it so much when you were younger you needed to come back for more. What's the matter? Doesn't Benjamin keep you in line like I did?"

"You hurt me, you bastard!" shouted Ellen.

"I'm going to hurt you again, you stupid wench!" he

shouted.

He wrestled her to the ground, trying to rip and tear at her clothing. Ellen wasn't a little girl this time, though, and she wasn't as easy to hold down or tie up. She bit Lester's finger as he tried to cover her mouth.

"Help me!" she screamed.

The struggle continued. Ellen was able to break free, but Lester grabbed her again.

"Help me!" she shouted again.

This time someone heard her. The front door opened. Ellen looked up and saw Sarah standing just inside the doorway.

"Do it!" she shouted.

Ellen was momentarily confused.

"Do it, Ellen! The old bastard deserves it!" Sarah shouted.

Ellen looked back at Lester and saw his throat just inches from her face. Suddenly she realized what Sarah wanted her to do.

She bit Lester.

"Finish him!" shouted Sarah.

Ellen ripped out Lester's trachea and spit it on the floor. She found she wasn't satisfied, though. She went after more of Lester. Sarah had to tackle her and hold her away from the body.

"No, Ellen! Don't! Don't!" shouted Sarah.

Ellen thrashed in Sarah's grip, trying to get away.

"Think of Jason and Ashley," Sarah said in Ellen's ear. "Calm down. Take deep breaths. Clear your mind!"

The commotion had drawn more people to the house. George walked inside and saw the carnage.

"Get the body out of here," Sarah told him. "Burn it!"

I started to get concerned when Ellen didn't come back

from her parents' house. I asked Josephine, Elizabeth's mother, to watch Jason and Ashley while I went to see what was keeping her. As I approached the house, I saw George dragging Lester's body out the front door.

"What's going on?" I asked George.

"Sarah told me to burn the body," replied George.

"Sarah?" I looked at Lester's shredded throat. "No, we don't want to burn it. That won't destroy all of the evidence. Let's feed him to the hogs instead."

"What?" replied George.

"Feed him to the hogs. They'll eat the bones and all, leaving no trace of Lester here. That way there won't be any evidence if anyone comes looking."

George and I carried Lester's body over to the hog pen and threw it in. It was feeding time and the hogs went wild on him. We went back in the house, where Sarah was still on the floor holding Ellen.

"What happened?" I asked.

"He tried to kill me," Ellen said, "just like he did when I was twelve."

I went over to Ellen and held her.

"I'm sorry," I said.

"It's okay. I got my revenge. That bastard won't be hurting anybody again. It's about time he did something good for me, anyway."

I looked over at Sarah. "Where have you been?" I asked her.

"I'll explain later. Let's just get Ellen out of here," she answered.

We all headed to back to the house.

Sarah had no more than walked through the door when she was ambushed by Jason. "Where have you been, Auntie Sarah?" he asked.

"Oh, here and there, little buddy. I've missed you," she

answered.

Ellen thanked Josephine for watching the kids, then picked up Ashley and took her to the rocker and began to nurse. I took a minute to reflect on the day's events, but seeing my family back together quickly relaxed me.

Chapter 19

A few hours passed. Jason and Ashley were both asleep. Sarah had made some coffee, so the three of us sat at the table and began to talk.

"So, Sarah, where have you been?" I asked.

"Soul searching," she said. "I had issues that I needed to come to terms with. The birth of Ashley made me realize my hopes were shot. Benjamin, I know we have a relationship like brother and sister, but deep down inside I've always wanted more than that between us. I've been jealous of your relationship with Ellen. I want what you guys have, so after the birth I had to get away and think. But the longer I was away from you both, the more it hurt. So I came back."

She looked nervously at Ellen.

"I'm glad you came back," Ellen said, "not only because you saved me or because you are here to help me with the kids. It's because I'm also jealous of you. I know that Benjamin and I have a good relationship, but you're the only one he will open up to and talk with. I'm jealous of that, but without you around it doesn't feel like we are a family. It's always been the three of us, and that's how I like it."

I was embarrassed and the girls knew it and began laughing at me. Their laughter didn't stop me from asking Ellen a question.

"So what was that about back at your parents' house?"

Ellen explained what Lester had done to her on her twelfth birthday.

"How would George know about it?"I asked.

"The one person I told was my cousin Mary. She was George's daughter. She must have told him before she died," explained Ellen.

I was so relieved to have Sarah back to help Ellen with the kids so I could concentrate on the harvest. All the men and older boys of the village were responsible for the harvest. We started in the south field with our sickles. We had about a quarter of the field done when some of the men began taking the grain to the storage bin. We worked from dusk until dawn for the next few days.

Finally, all the harvesting was done and it came time for the corn and beans to be milled into meal for later use. We were about halfway done with the milling process when the skies opened and it all let loose. It rained for days: ten of them, to be exact. The stream that ran beside our village swelled over its banks and flooded our grain storage bins. By the time the water receded, all the beans and corn that hadn't been milled were ruined. The crops were covered in mold. We didn't just lose half of our harvest, we also lost all the seed for the next season.

I ran into Sarah in the park. "What are we going to do?" I asked.

"We need to go after bigger game," she replied. "The three of us could work together and take down a deer or two. That would help."

"We could, but there has been so much settlement around here that I'm afraid we will have more incidents like Ellen's father," I said.

"Our only other option is to move the village to an uninhabited area. Or we can learn to share our hunting grounds peacefully," she said.

I liked our village where it was, and besides the one incident, we had co-existed with the humans very well. I was a little less stressed after talking to Sarah.

"I'm going home," I said. "Are you coming with me?"

"I'll be home later," she replied.

I walked through the door and was met by Ellen. "We have a problem," she said.

I sighed. "What now?"

"I haven't seen you much lately…and the kids are in bed."

"I'm too tired for that," I replied.

"That's not what I was talking about. How about you and I go outside and watch the sunset together," she said.

"That sounds good to me," I replied.

We went outside on the porch and watched the sunset. About ten minutes later, we could make out a silhouette walking up the lane. It was Sarah, walking slowly with her head down. We waited for her to come onto the porch.

"What's wrong, Sarah?" asked Ellen.

"It's just me," replied Sarah.

Ellen gave me a look. I went into the house so the two of them could have a discussion.

"Come on, Sarah, you can talk to me," Ellen said. "What's wrong?"

"I know we've had this discussion before, but I can't get over my feelings for Benjamin. I've been thinking it might be best if I just left."

Ellen replied, "I don't want you to leave, and neither does Benjamin. Or Jason. What can I do to help?"

"I can't ask you for it, Ellen. It just isn't right," replied Sarah.

"Sarah, I'm so gracious for everything you have done for me, and for my family. You can ask me for anything."

"No, I can't. I'll be fine. I'm going to bed," replied Sarah.

Whatever was bothering Sarah that night, it seemed to heal with time. It was almost New Year's and things were going well. The weather had been excellent, which helped us hunt and store food. That all changed the night of New Year's Eve; it had nothing to do with the weather but with the return of Martin, the man who had told us about horseless carriages on the east coast.

"The rains ruined over two-thirds of our harvest, and hunting is not putting enough food on the table. I'm begging you to help," he told me.

"I'll see what I can do," I told him. "Let's discuss it over supper."

We went in the house and sat down for supper. Ellen served us as we discussed the situation.

"We lost almost half of our crops, too," I told him.

"I'll understand if you can't help us out," he replied. "We've been lucky so far with a mild winter. But when the snow flies, I'm afraid my village will starve."

I thought back to the winter when so many of our villagers starved and how much of a disaster it was for us.

"We can help at least a little," I said. "You stay here tonight, and in the morning we will put some food together for you to take back to your village."

"Thank you. I walked here, though. I have no way to carry much back to the village with me."

I remembered Lester's wagon and horses at the farm.

"That won't be a problem. We have a wagon and some horses for you to use."

I awoke early in the morning. I took Martin to the farm for the horses and wagon.

"I don't know how I can ever thank you enough, Benjamin," he said.

I replied, "You never know. Next year we may need your help."

We got the horses hooked up to the wagon, then met up with Ellen and Sarah at the smokehouse. We loaded a few barrels of cornmeal onto the wagon along with some containers of jerky. While we were at the farm we had slaughtered a few hogs; we gutted them out at the smokehouse and re-loaded them onto the wagon.

"I hope this will help you out," I told him.

"Thank you all very much," Martin said as he climbed into the captain seat of the wagon. He headed on his way to the village. We all waved to him as he disappeared in the distance.

Chapter 20

It made me feel good inside to help Martin. I had a big smile on my face when I felt something hit my nose. It was the first snowflake of the year. It began to come down pretty hard. The three of us played in it like little kids, throwing snowballs and making snow angels. Time got away from us, and before we knew it there was about four inches of snow on the ground. We headed back to the house.

We walked in the door and I was greeted by Jason.

"Daddy, can we go sledding?" he asked.

I looked at Ellen.

"Why don't you and Sarah take him sledding?" she said. "I'll stay here with Ashley."

Sarah got Jason dressed while I went out and got his sled. They met me by the steps. Jason hopped on his sled and I pulled him as Sarah pelted me with snowballs. We went to a big hill by the stream. Jason would slide down on his sled while Sarah and I slid down any way we could.

After one downhill tumble, Sarah somehow ended up on top of me. In the heat of the moment, we kissed. I had never felt anything like the emotion that ran through me. I didn't want it to end, but reality struck quickly and she got up off me. We looked at Jason, who had a strange look on his face. Sarah pleaded with him not to tell Ellen. She had to bribe him with an offer of cookies before he promised to keep the secret.

Ellen came into the kitchen as we were taking off our coats.

"Did you have fun?" she asked.

Jason shouted, "Yes, Mommy, and guess what."

I thought he was going to tell her right there.

"Sarah is going to make cookies!" he finished.

I had a relieved look on my face and so did Sarah. I took Jason into his room to get warm clothes on him while Ellen went back to check on Ashley and Sarah got things together to make cookies.

I took Jason into the family room and sat in front of the fire. Ellen was nursing Ashley in the rocker. Sarah finished mixing the cookie dough, put the cookies into the oven, and joined us. Jason got off my lap and went and sat on Sarah's lap. He planted a big wet kiss on Sarah's lips. This caught Sarah off guard.

"Is that for making cookies?" Sarah asked him.

Jason just smiled.

After sharing some nice warm cookies, it was soon time for bed. It wasn't long before Sarah made her way into my dreams, her body pressed against mine. I woke up in a cold sweat. I snuggled up to Ellen, trying to clear my head, and went back to sleep.

In the morning, we had about eighteen inches of snow on the ground. I wondered if Martin had made it back to his village safely. Ellen had come out on the porch and put her hands on my shoulders.

"What's wrong?" she asked.

"I'm worried about Martin," I told her.

"Why don't you and Sarah go and check on him?" she said.

I didn't want to go anywhere with Sarah by myself after the dreams I had the previous night and the events of the previous day.

"Go and check on who?" came from the front door.

"Sarah, Benjamin is worried if Martin made it back to his village. I think you two should go and check," Ellen said.

"That sounds like a good idea," replied Sarah.

I reluctantly agreed. Sarah and I headed out to the edge of the village, changed into wolf form, and followed the scent of the horses. We tracked for several hours until we could smell the village ahead. Then we changed back to human form and headed into the village. It wasn't hard to pick up Martin's scent and figure out which house was his. Sarah and I went up to his door and knocked.

"Benjamin!" Martin said when he opened the door. "Sarah! What are you two doing here?"

"We wanted to make sure you made it through the snow," I said.

"What smells so good?" Sarah added.

"The women are preparing a meal in the community building," he replied. "Why don't you two stay and be my guests?"

"Okay," I said.

"My wife is already over there, so let's go," he said.

We headed over to the community building. On our way, Sarah began to act like something was bothering her.

"Please excuse me," she said. "I'm not feeling well. I'll be back in a little bit."

Martin and I entered the community building. All the villagers were in there. They had just finished saying grace. We sat down and had started eating when Sarah walked in and came up to me.

"Benjamin, we need to go," she said. "I'm not feeling well and want to get home."

I thanked Martin for dinner and headed out with Sarah.

"What's going on?" I asked.

"Use your nose," she said.

I took a big whiff.

"Did you smell it?" she asked.

"Elizabeth," I said. "I do smell her."

"Did you see her in the community building?" she asked.

"No. I didn't see her, nor did I smell her," I said.

"I know she's around here somewhere, but I don't know where. We need to come back when the weather clears so we can investigate."

The winter continued. Ellen and I enjoyed a wonderful Valentine's Day. Sarah watched the kids for us while we had dinner together and some alone time. That night, the snow began to fall, the wind picked up, and the temperature fell well below freezing.

The next morning I went out to get firewood. I had to push the snow to get out of the back door. Nearly eighteen inches of snow had fallen, and drifts were up to four feet high.

I made my way through the drifting snow. The wind was howling as it blew. I made my way to the woodpile and began several trips back and forth. I finally had enough wood piled on the back porch to make it through a couple of days, hoping by then the weather would pass by. I went back into the house and had some coffee to warm up. I still had to go to the farm and tend to the hogs. I was sitting at the table when Sarah sat down with me.

"I want to go with you, to help tend to the hogs," she

said.

"I don't need you to come with me," I told her.

She was persistent. "I insist."

Ellen walked into the kitchen, and she sided with Sarah.

"I think that would be a good idea," Ellen said.

I knew it would be a waste of time to argue, so I agreed to let Sarah come alone with me to tend to the hogs. I finished my coffee and got dressed and ready to go outside. Sarah was already waiting for me on the porch.

"Isn't the snow beautiful?" she said.

"It's pretty, but we could do without all this wind," I told her.

We made it to the farm with no incident. We had to dig our way into the barn to get to the hogs. Sarah thought it would be funny as we were digging to keep throwing her snow on me. So I threw it back at her.

We finally made our way into the barn. We had just made it to the hogs when we heard the door blow shut. We barely noticed as we fed the hogs and laid out straw for them. We then started to clean out the area in the barn where the hogs were.

When we were finished and tried to leave the barn, I pushed but the door wouldn't budge.

"Come over here and help me push, Sarah," I said.

The two of us pushed on the door. We still couldn't get it to budge. We tried several times with no luck. All the other doors had been locked from the outside, so there was no other way out. We kept trying to open the door until we were both too exhausted to try anymore. We sat down to rest.

Ellen was making lunch, expecting us back anytime. She rounded Jason up and sat him at the table.

"Dad and Sarah should be home anytime now," she

told him.

"Can I play in the snow after lunch, Mommy?" Jason asked.

Ellen looked out the window. "Probably not today, honey. It's still snowing and the wind is still blowing really hard."

Ellen looked out the window again.

"Well, let's go ahead and eat. Dad and Sarah must be getting held up by the weather," she told Jason.

Sarah and I were struggling to stay warm in the barn. We were both shivering. We tried again to get the door open, but it was useless. We couldn't budge it at all. I got the bright idea that maybe I should get a running start at it. I backed up fifteen steps away from the door. I began to run at the door, lowered my shoulder, and rammed right into it. I ended up on the floor with some awful pain in my shoulder.

Sarah came over to me. "Are you okay?" she asked.

"My shoulder," I said. "It's burning and hurts really bad. I think I tore something or dislocated it."

Sarah took a couple burlap feed bags and made a sling for my arm to support my shoulder.

"I need to find us a way out of here," she said.

She looked around the whole barn and finally found a small hole in one wall.

"I think I can get through that if I change," she told me.

"I don't know," I told her. "It looks pretty small."

"We don't have any other choice but to freeze to death in here. When I get out I can dig the door out and get it open for you."

I finally agreed that it was our only option. Sarah took her wolf form and tried to squeeze out through the little hole in the wall. Like I thought, the hole was too small, but she was bound and determined to get us out. She pulled her head back into the barn to dig. She was digging hard and fast, but the ground was frozen, inhibiting her progress. Finally, she was able to get through the hole.

Over an hour passed and still Sarah hadn't opened the barn door for me. I decided to try to get out the hole myself. I changed into a wolf and went to the hole. It was a tight fit, but I finally managed to squeeze my way out.

I limped my way out and there was Sarah, lying motionless in the snow. Her breathing was shallow. I nudged her with my nose to get a response but there wasn't much of one. She could barely lift her head. I lay down beside her to try to warm her up.

As darkness fell, Ellen was worried about us. She had put Ashley and Jason down for a nap. Since the wind and snow had slowed, she decided to try to find us. She left the kids at home and headed into the elements.

"Benjamin!" she called. "Sarah! Where are you?"

There was no response. She yelled again.

This time she got a response; it was her Uncle George.

"What's going on, Ellen?" he asked.

"Benjamin and Sarah went earlier to tend to the hogs and they aren't back yet," she said.

"Who's with the kids?" he asked.

"Nobody."

"You go back to your house," George told her. "I'll go find them."

Sarah and I were snuggled up in a ball, sharing our warmth. She was becoming a little more active. I looked and saw a figure in the distance, and I could make out a muffled voice. It sounded familiar.

As the figure came closer, I could make out that it was

George. I changed back into human form and yelled for him.

"Benjamin! Is that you?" he yelled to me.

"Yes it is!" I yelled back.

George stepped up his pace and headed toward us. Sarah had finally recovered enough to change back into human form, but she was still very weak.

George came over to us. "What's going on?" he asked.

I explained, "We got stuck in the barn. The snow must have blown back in front of the door."

George helped Sarah up and the three of us walked to the front of the barn. To our amazement, there was no snow in front of the door, but there was a log that had been dragged there.

"Someone didn't want us to get out," I said.

Ellen was pacing, wearing a trail into the kitchen floor, when she finally saw the lantern light coming up the lane. She opened the door and waited on the porch for us to arrive. When we came onto to the porch, she came out and gave me a big hug, jarring my shoulder.

"Ouch!" I shouted.

"What's wrong, Benjamin?" Ellen asked.

"My shoulder," I replied. "I tore something or dislocated it at the farm."

George suggested, "Maybe we should go in and get warm."

We all went into the house. Ellen made coffee while George, Sarah, and I huddled around the fire.

I asked Sarah, "What happened to you?"

"I got through the hole and was on my way to the door when I was struck in the back of the head with something. It must have knocked me out. I vaguely remember you coming up to me."

"Who would've done something like that to us?" I asked.

"I have an idea, but I need to do some investigation," said Sarah.

"Who do you think it was?" I asked.

Sarah was getting ready to answer my question but fell silent when Ellen came in with the coffee.

When the coffee was gone, all of Ellen's attention turned to me and my shoulder. She soaked some towels in hot water and then laid them across my shoulder. Then she took some other cloth and made a sling for my shoulder.

In the process of being bandaged up, I lost track of what Sarah and I had been talking about. Jason came out of his room and wanted his Auntie Sarah. George decided it was time to leave for home. It wasn't much longer and we turned in for the night.

In the morning, my shoulder still hurt like the dickens. I could barely move it. I struggled getting out of bed. Ellen assisted me and helped me get dressed. I felt like a helpless child.

I made my way into the kitchen and watched Ellen make breakfast. About half an hour later, Sarah finally came out of her room. She was rubbing her neck.

"My neck sure is stiff this morning," she said.

Ellen went over by the fire, soaked a towel in the hot water, then wrung it out and took it over to Sarah. She placed the towel on the back of Sarah's neck.

"Oh, that feels so good," Sarah said. "Thanks."

"You're welcome," Ellen replied.

Ellen then turned her attention back to breakfast. Sarah and I could do nothing but watch Ellen do all the work. Jason then came running into the kitchen and went right up to Sarah.

"What's that on your neck, Auntie Sarah?" he asked.

"Just a hot towel," Sarah answered.

"What for?"

"Auntie Sarah hurt her neck yesterday," she replied.

"How?" he asked.

Before Sarah could answer Jason, I remembered our conversation from the night before.

So who do you think did it?" I asked Sarah.

"Believe it or not, I think it was Elizabeth," she replied.

"Why would Elizabeth do something like that?" I asked.

"Food," Sarah replied. "Easy food."

As I thought about it, I started to see Sarah's point. We had picked up Elizabeth's scent over at Martin's village, after all. I wanted to go try to find her, but Sarah and I were in no shape for it.

After breakfast it was time to tend to the chores. It was a good thing I had already stocked up on firewood for a few days. Ellen went out and tended to all the chores around the house, leaving Sarah and me in the house to entertain the kids. Ashley was sleeping, but Jason was a little terror, getting into everything.

"Daddy, let's play this," he would say. Then he would go and get something else out. Before I knew it he had all his toys strewn all over the floor. I was struggling to keep up with him. Sarah finally came back into the family room after trying to sleep off a headache.

"Does your head feel any better?" I asked her.

"A little bit. At least I can stand to have my eyes open," she said.

Sarah sat down in the rocker and watched as I struggled to keep up with Jason. She finally grabbed Jason and held him in the chair.

"You better pick up your toys, or the one-armed pirate is going to come and get you," she told him.

Jason laughed and said, "No, he won't."

"Then don't pick up your toys and we'll see," she said.

I was in with Ashley when Sarah told Jason about the pirate. I tied some material together over my head like a bandanna and put a patch on my eye. I went into the family room.

"Ahoy there, me mateys," I said.

Jason laughed.

"I'm the one-armed pirate here to get any little boys who don't pick up their booty," I said.

Jason was still laughing.

"Well, if you don't want to cooperate, I'll make you walk the plank and swim with the fishes," I said.

Sarah whispered in Jason ear. "The fishes like fresh meat," she told him.

Jason jumped off of Sarah's lap and started picking up his toys. "I don't want the fishes to eat me," he kept repeating. He had just finished picking up as Ellen walked through the front door.

"Chores are all done. How'd things go in here?" she asked.

"Fine," Sarah and I replied at the same time.

Ellen took off her boots and her layers of clothes and sat down for some coffee. Sarah and I joined her.

"How are you two feeling?" Ellen asked us.

"I'm fine," replied Sarah.

"I can't stand to move my arm," I said. "I should go see Dr. Morris and get something for the pain."

"I'll go with you," Sarah said. "I'll have him check me out too."

The two of us got our winter clothes on and headed out. We trudged through the snow to Dr. Morris's house. We knocked on the door; he answered and let us in.

"What brings you two here on such a lovely day?" he

asked.

Sarah explained to him first.

"Someone hit me in the back of the head and neck area yesterday while we were tending to the hogs at Ellen's parents' old farm. I've had a headache ever since."

Dr. Morris did some tests on Sarah. He checked her eyes and asked her some questions.

"Looks like you may have a slight concussion. You should feel better in a day or so," he said.

He then turned to me.

"What's going on with you today, Benjamin?" he asked.

I told him about ramming into the barn door and the pain I'd had in my shoulder ever since.

He took my arm, raised it above my head, and pushed my shoulder back into place. We heard a loud popping noise.

"That should help, Benjamin, but I think you should take it easy for a couple of weeks," he said.

"I can't take it easy for a few weeks," I told him.

"You must take it easy. I'm afraid you may have partially torn your rotator cuff. If you don't take it easy, we may have to operate on it."

I didn't want to have surgery so I agreed to take it easy.

"Can I have something for the pain?" I asked him.

He handed me some pills.

"These are opium. They will help you relax and ease the pain, but don't take more than two a day," he told me.

Chapter 21

"So what did Dr. Morris have to say?" Ellen asked as Sarah and I walked in.

Sarah replied, "I have a slight concussion and should be fine in a day or two, but Benjamin is a different story."

Ellen looked at me.

"I have a partially torn rotator cuff," I said. "I need to take it easy for a few weeks. He said if I didn't, I could injure it enough that he would have to do surgery."

"That isn't good," Ellen said. "How are we going to manage?"

"He also put me on opium. He said it would help relax me and help with the pain. I'm supposed to take only two a day, no more."

"Well, it's only a few weeks. Sarah and I can manage the chores," Ellen said.

After supper, I took my first opium pill. Within an hour, I was in a very relaxed state. Sarah had managed to sneak a nap in after lunch and she was busy helping Ellen finish the chores. The evening flew by for me. The opium pretty much wiped me out. I didn't have any pain but my mind was in a haze. I couldn't think straight and just felt funny. I vaguely remember being up for a few hours during the evening but I couldn't tell you what went on. Ellen joined me in bed later that evening; she must have been tired because she barely moved.

I was sound asleep when a commotion awoke me. I looked out the window and noticed the glow of fire near our grain storage. I tried to get up out of bed but couldn't. Sarah ran into our room.

"The grain bin is on fire!" she screamed.

This woke Ellen up and the two of them helped me out of bed. I slipped into my winter clothes and headed out to the storage bin. Most of the villagers were already there, trying to control the fire. I felt helpless as I watched the others working frantically. Ellen and Sarah joined them in fighting the fire. Eventually they managed to put the fire out, but it was a total loss. All of our grain for the rest of the year was destroyed. This was a big blow to our village. I began to cry.

"I failed us," I cried.

Ellen came over to me and put her arm around me. "It's not your fault," she said. "You can't control everything, no matter how hard you try."

I just buried my head into her shoulder and let the tears stream down.

Sarah had been investigating the scene. She came over to where Ellen and I were standing.

"This was no accident," she told us.

"Why do you think that?" asked Ellen.

"I smelled a familiar smell. I believe that it was Martin that did this."

I lifted my head from Ellen's shoulder. "Martin wouldn't have done something like this to us," I said. "Not after we helped him out."

"He wasn't in this on his own," Sarah replied. "Use

your nose. There are a few unfamiliar scents here too."

"I would if I could. I'm catching a cold and my nose is stuffy," I told her.

Ellen sniffed the air.

"What am I looking for?" she asked.

"Take another big whiff. See if you smell Martin," replied Sarah.

Ellen took another big whiff. "I can smell him," she said.

Since there wasn't anything else we could do, we headed back home. I went back to bed as Ellen and Sarah stayed up to work out a plan.

"We need to go and get answers," Ellen said.

"Hold on a moment. You aren't going anywhere," Sarah told Ellen.

"Since Benjamin is out of commission, I'm in charge around here."

"What do you mean, you're in charge around here?" exclaimed Sarah.

"Benjamin is the alpha and I'm his wife. Since he is out of commission, I'm in charge."

"That may be right, but you are in no shape to be leading anything," replied Sarah.

This angered Ellen. "In shape? I'll show you," she said. "I'll go to Martin's village all by myself and get answers!" shouted Ellen.

Ellen stormed out the door.

Sarah waited for Ellen to come back in after having a chance to cool off. After an hour, though, Ellen still hadn't returned. Ashley was crying for her feeding and Jason wanted to eat also. Sarah tended to the children's needs. She made Jason something to eat and fed Ashley some corn mush cereal. She then came into my room.

"Benjamin!" she shouted. "Wake up!"

I rolled over and moaned a little. Sarah began bouncing the mattress to try to wake me. I finally couldn't stand it anymore and woke up.

"What's your problem?" I asked her.

"Ellen left about two hours ago and she hasn't come back yet," she told me.

"Why did she leave?"

"She told me that she was in charge and that she was going to get to the bottom of the problem at Martin's village."

"Why did you let her go? You know she has to be here for the kids. What were you thinking, Sarah?"

Sarah tried to explain but I interrupted her, shouting, "Go find her, and don't come back until you do!"

"What about the kids?" she said. "You're in no shape to watch them."

"I'll manage."

"I'm not leaving the kids home alone with you. That medication has you sleeping the day away, and the kids don't need that. Ellen can take care of herself. The kids can't, and that's where I draw the line." She stormed out of the bedroom before I could say another word.

Ellen had changed into wolf form and headed toward Martin's village. She was making pretty good time. She was about a half a mile away from the village when something hit her and everything went dark.

When she regained consciousness, she was in a cage. She tried to chew her way out, but it was useless. The wire was too hard for her to chew through. She began digging, trying to get under the fence, but the ground was frozen. She then tried jumping the fence. She almost made it; she just needed a little more speed. She backed up as far as she could, got a running start, and was able to clear the fence.

She took off running. But she also drew the attention of the person that had captured her. He came running out of his house with his gun and began shooting at her. Ellen dodged the bullets, looking for anything to take cover under. She finally found a hole under some brush and scrambled into it. She could hear the man outside the hole.

"You're safe now," he said, "but I'll be back with a trap."

Ellen knew she needed to make a break for it as soon as the man left. She waited patiently until the man's scent faded. She peeked her head out of the hole and saw the coast was clear. She ran off as fast as she could, but in the commotion, she had lost her sense of direction.

It was getting dark and Sarah was growing more and more concerned that Ellen hadn't made it back home yet. She decided to go and get Josephine to watch the kids while she went out to find Ellen. Sarah and Josephine walked into the house just as Ashley was beginning to cry.

"Great timing," laughed Josephine.

"No time to laugh. I have to go," said Sarah.

Sarah headed out the door, changed into wolf form, and tracked Ellen. She tracked her to about a half a mile from the village when the scent disappeared. Sarah changed back into her human form to do a little investigation. She looked around in the snow and noticed a spot in the snow shaped like something had lain there. She then noticed footprints leading to and away from it.

"I bet these tracks will lead me to Ellen," she said to herself.

Sarah changed back into wolf form and followed the scent that accompanied the tracks. It led her to a house just outside the village. She then rediscovered Ellen's scent by a cage. She followed the scent into a hole under some brush. From there she continued to follow the scent.

It was now very dark and cold. Sarah was determined to find Ellen, though, so she kept on tracking long into the night.

Ellen was panicking; she couldn't find any familiar scents or scenery. She was getting tired and cold. She tried to locate a suitable shelter, but shelter was rare. She finally found a brush pile of pine that she could nestle under to get out of the weather.

Meanwhile, Sarah continued to track Ellen. The scent was getting stronger and stronger, so she knew she wasn't too far away. She let out a loud howl.

The howl awoke Ellen, who recognized it from nights of hunting with the pack. She let out her own howl in response.

Sarah heard the reply and picked up her pace toward the howl. Ellen came out of her shelter and headed toward the direction of Sarah's howl. Ellen was able to see Sarah in the distance. She waited there until Sarah joined her. They both turned into human form.

"How did you wind up way out here?" asked Sarah.

Ellen explained what had happened, and how she had found some meager shelter after her escape.

"We need to go back to that shelter and spend the rest of the night there," Sarah said. "We are too far away from home to get back there tonight."

"Who's watching the kids?" asked Ellen.

"Josephine. You should have thought about that before you stormed off, though!"

"I know."

They had been asleep for a few hours when they were awoken by a bloodcurdling howl. They both were shaking in their fur. The howl came again, too close for comfort.

All they could do was make a run for it.

They burst from their shelter and began to run. Sarah looked back and saw a lycan hot on their tails. The brush became very thick and was hard to maneuver through. Ellen and Sarah ran side by side and stride for stride until Ellen got hung up in some really thick brush. Sarah heard a loud yelp. She turned around to see Ellen trying to get free from the brush. Sarah turned back and tried to help.

The lycan was getting closer. Sarah charged at it to get its attention, but it ignored her and headed toward Ellen. Sarah then went after the lycan from behind and bit its back leg. The lycan just threw her off his leg.

Sarah had given Ellen enough time to get out of the brush, but all the struggling had exhausted her. She tried to run as fast as she could, but she wasn't fast enough to avoid the lycan. Sarah watched in horror as the lycan caught Ellen with a swipe of its claws. Ellen let out a gut-wrenching yelp. Sarah jumped on the lycan and bit it on the back of the neck. This allowed Ellen to crawl down a hole, and Sarah followed. The lycan dug until the sun came up about an hour later, trying to get to them, but eventually left empty-handed.

Sarah spent that hour licking the blood coming from Ellen's wound, trying to help it clot. Ellen was lying motionless and breathing shallowly. As soon as Sarah saw sunlight poking through the hole she went back aboveground and changed into human form. She looked around and could see smoke a short distance away. She reached down and helped Ellen out of the hole.

As Ellen changed into human form, Sarah could see the damage the lycan had done to her. Ellen was very pale and had a huge laceration running up her right side. Sarah wrapped Ellen in as many clothes as she could to keep her warm.

"There's a village right over there, about a mile away," Sarah said. "I'm going to get help."

"Don't worry about me," Ellen replied. "It's too late. Please just make it home to take care of my family."

"You'll be fine, Ellen, I promise." With that, Sarah headed toward the village as fast as she could. She went up to the first house she saw and pounded on the door.

"Help me! Help me!" she shouted.

A woman came to the door.

"You have to help me. My friend has been injured!" Sarah shouted.

The woman's husband came to the door. "Let me get dressed and I'll be right there," he said.

The woman let Sarah in and they waited as the man got his winter clothes on.

"Do you have a sled?" Sarah asked.

"It's in the barn. It's on the way," the man replied.

He finished getting dressed, then he and Sarah went out to the barn for the sled. When they got back to Ellen, she wasn't in very good shape. She was unconscious and barely breathing. Sarah and the man loaded her on the sled and dragged her back to the house. The woman of the house had already gone to get the village doctor, who was waiting on the porch as Sarah and the man brought Ellen in. The doctor took a look at Ellen.

"It doesn't look very good," he said. "She has lost a lot of blood and is in shock. It's too late for me to do anything for her. I'm sorry."

Sarah fell to her knees, crying. "Please don't take her, God. Take me instead!"

Sarah went over and cradled Ellen's head in her lap as Ellen gasped her last breath. Sarah cried harder.

"I'm so sorry, Ellen! I'm sorry!"

The woman placed her hands on Sarah's shoulders.

"You did everything you could," she said.

"Thank you for everything," replied Sarah. She grabbed the ropes to the sled and headed out from the village.

Chapter 22

I hadn't taken any opium that morning, so I was aware enough to know that something wasn't right.

"Where are Sarah and Ellen?" I asked Josephine.

"Sarah came and got me last night saying that she needed to find Ellen," she told me. "I've been here all night."

"You said you were here all night?" I asked.

"Yes," replied Josephine.

My shoulder was feeling better but I knew there was no way I could go and look for them. I decided to give them until dark to get home before I would attempt a search.

Josephine had made some coffee. "Did you know that Elizabeth was here the other day?" she asked me.

"No, I didn't," I replied. "Why didn't you say something to me about it?"

"Because she isn't right. The man she brought back with her gave me a strange feeling."

"Can you explain it to me?" I asked.

"I don't know. He just…bothered me. And the smell was something awful."

I thought for a moment. That's when I realized how

lost I was without Sarah there to figure things out for me.

"I'll have you talk to Sarah when she gets back," I told her.

"I don't think Ellen and Sarah are going to make it back. He wants to hurt you," Josephine said.

"Have you been drinking, Josephine?" I asked.

"Not when I'm watching your kids," she replied.

This got me thinking.

Sarah pulled the sled with Ellen's body on it until she was far enough away from the village to change into a wolf. Then she stepped into the ropes of the sled so they pulled across her chest, and she guided it that way. She continued on her way back home.

I spent as much time as I could with Jason so he wouldn't ask me every five minutes where Ellen was. It was getting late in the evening and I was growing more and more concerned that she and Sarah weren't back yet. I hadn't forgotten what Josephine said to me earlier. I wondered why Elizabeth would stop by and not stay, and who the man was that had come with her.

Josephine had made supper; I decided to look out the window before I sat down to eat. I looked out into the dark with the moonlight reflecting off the snow, but I didn't see anything. I just played with my food. My worry overrode any hunger I might have had. I was ready to excuse myself from the table when I heard a faint howl in the distance. A few moments later I heard it again.

I knew it was Sarah. I got up from the table and ran outside. I could see the silhouette of a wolf in the distance. Then suddenly it changed to a woman and collapsed to the ground. I went out to help. Sarah looked at me.

"I'm sorry, Benjamin," she said before she passed out.

The adrenaline kicked in and the pain in my shoulder was gone. I picked Sarah up and carried her into the house. I laid her on the floor in front of the fire. Then I went out and pulled the sled into the barn. I didn't even bother to look under the covers; I was too concerned about Sarah.

I went back into the house, warmed up some towels, and placed them on Sarah's head. Josephine took Jason and Ashley to their rooms. I slowly took Sarah's clothes off and covered her naked body with a warm blanket. I held her cold hand.

"Please don't die," I told her.

I kept rubbing her hand, trying to stimulate her. She finally started to come around. "We have to get Ellen," she mumbled. She then fell back asleep. I sat up with her in front of the fire, adding logs whenever the flame started dying out. I had just fallen asleep when I was awoken abruptly.

"Where's Ellen? We have to get Ellen!" Sarah shouted. She was running around the house naked in a panic. She came up to me.

"What did you do with Ellen?" she asked me.

"Ellen wasn't with you," I said. "You were by yourself with a sled."

"The sled. Ellen was on the sled!"

Sarah put some clothes on and the two of us headed out to the barn. Sarah approached it slowly.

"I'm sorry, Benjamin," she said as she lifted the covers up.

I couldn't believe it. There was Ellen, lying under the blankets. I fell to my knees next to her, crying. I grabbed her hand, which was ice cold. I kept thinking of the time I met her and how beautiful she was, and how she had blessed me with two beautiful children. The pain in my heart was soon replaced with anger. I lashed out at Sarah.

"How could you let this happen to her? I told you to go after her earlier yesterday. Why didn't you obey? I can't believe you let your feelings for me interfere with your judgment. I don't think any amount of jealousy is worth this!"

Sarah put her head down. "It wasn't my fault," she said in a soft voice.

"Whatever!" I shouted back at her.

Sarah took off into the house. I spent the night in the barn with Ellen.

Dawn was approaching as I kneeled motionless beside Ellen's cold, motionless body, holding her ice-cold hand for the last time. I got up and headed out of the barn. As I looked back, reality hit me. The tears poured down my face as I walked into the quiet house. I didn't get too far inside before I noticed Sarah at the table.

"Have you been here all night?" I asked her.

"Yes," she replied. "I've been waiting for you to walk through the door."

"Why?"

"Because you need to understand. It wasn't my fault," she said.

I let it go at that. I went to my empty bed and lay down in it. It wasn't long before Sarah came into the room.

"Benjamin, as long as you need me to help with the kids, I will be here, but please don't treat me like a murderer. There was nothing I could do to save her," she said.

I got out of bed and got right into Sarah's face. "If you would have gone when I told you to, this wouldn't have happened!" I shouted.

"Who would have watched the kids? You weren't in any shape to do it. Ellen was old enough to make her own decision to go. You need to understand that. I know that you are grieving right now, and you're taking your anger out on me. Just understand, I'm grieving too, but someone needs to be strong for the kids. Benjamin, if you need me, I'll be here."

Sarah went back into the kitchen. Jason came out and joined her.

"Good morning, buddy," she said.

"Where's Mommy?" he asked.

Sarah didn't know quite how to answer Jason. "Mommy is still gone," she said. "We don't know when she'll be back."

I slept for a few hours and took some time to think about the whole situation. I went out to the living room and saw Sarah and Jason playing. Sarah looked up at me but continued playing with Jason. I put my winter clothes on and went outside. I walked to the park and sat on the bench were Ellen and I would sit quite a bit.

"Why did I have to put this curse upon her?" I said to myself.

I sat in the park until I was too cold. I decided to go to George's house to inform him of the bad news. I walked up and knocked on his door.

"Benjamin, what are you doing here?" he asked.

I tried to tell him but the words just wouldn't come out.

"Are you okay, Benjamin? What's wrong?"

I tried again but still couldn't get the words out. I could feel my lip begin to quiver.

"Come in, Benjamin, and get warmed up," he told me.

I followed him into his house, where he sat me in front of the fire.

"What's going on?" he asked me again.

I mustered up all the strength I had inside and opened my mouth. "Ellen's dead," I said.

I must not have said it very loud.

"Benjamin, you're going to have to speak up," George said. "I can't make out what you're saying."

"Ellen is dead," I repeated.

"Not her too," replied George. "How did it happen?"

"She took it upon herself to go and check Martin's village on the hunch that Elizabeth was there," I told him.

George sat down in his chair and tears began to well up in his eyes. I placed a hand on his shoulder to try to comfort him. As I did so, I could feel a big lump building in my throat. I began to cry and George joined me. For several minutes we both let our emotions go. Eventually George spoke to me.

"I can't do another one," he said.

I told him, "Don't worry. She was my wife. I'll handle it."

"I'm sorry, Benjamin. If there is anything else I can do for you I'll be glad to help."

I thanked him as I headed out the door.

When I got home, the first place I went was the barn. I sat beside Ellen for a while.

"Why did you have to go?" I asked her. "It should have been Sarah!"

I heard the barn door close. I looked around but couldn't find anything that would have pushed it shut. I stayed in the barn for another fifteen minutes, and then I went in the house.

Sarah and Jason were eating supper. I sat down and joined them. As we ate, Sarah was silent. I figured it was just the stress of Ellen's death, so I let her be.

After supper I went into the family room with Jason and played with him while Sarah took Ashley and tended to her.

"Auntie Sarah said Mommy is in Heaven," Jason said. This caught me off guard.

"She also told me that Mommy will always be watching over me," he added.

I was at a loss for words, and I could feel that lump building in my throat again. "I'll be right back, buddy," I told him.

I headed through the kitchen and outside to the porch. I began to cry. A few minutes later, Sarah came outside after me. I turned around to see her just as she came out the door.

"Why did you tell him that?" I shouted at her.

"Did you want me to lie to him and keep his hopes up that Ellen was going to walk in the door any time?" she shouted back.

"No, I just wanted to tell him myself," I said.

"I'm sorry, Benjamin. I didn't know where your head was, I just thought I would do it so you wouldn't have to worry about it."

I was about to say something else when we noticed Jason looking out the window at us. "I'll take care of him," Sarah said as she went back in the house.

I stayed out on the porch for a while longer to collect my thoughts and my emotions. I had just buried my father-in-law a few months ago, and now I had to bury my wife. I had so much on my mind that would soon come back to haunt me.

We buried Ellen on the hardest day of my life. As the first shovelful of dirt was thrown on her casket, my emotions ran wild. Sarah tried to comfort me, but I found I couldn't open up to her as I had in the past. I blamed her for Ellen's death and that put a dent in our relationship. Sarah was taking care of Ashley the best she could, though; I could see that she was treating her as her own.

Chapter 23

The day after we buried Ellen, I met with the other men of the village to discuss our predicament of seed for the coming planting season.

I asked Luke, "Can we borrow a goat from you to use for Ashley?"

He replied, "Benjamin, you can have one if you need it. Do you need any other help?"

"Not right now. Just the goat."

We decided that I should take some others with me and go to a neighboring village to ask for seed. We decided that we would leave in two days, so we would be back before the full moon. The meeting adjourned and I headed to Luke's house to get a goat.

"Are you sure you don't need any other help?" he asked.

"I'm sure," I told him.

We went to his barn and put some rope around a goat's neck. I led her out of the barn, thanking Luke as I left his barnyard.

He shouted, "Let me know if I can help any other way!"

I waved to acknowledge that I heard him and headed

home. I walked into the house as Sarah was finishing supper.

"I'm leaving in two days to find a village that we may let us borrow seed for this spring planting," I told her.

"Did you get a goat?" she asked.

"She's in the barn. Can I trust you to take care of him?"

Sarah threw down her towel and stormed out the door. I ate supper and cleaned up, then went outside to see where Sarah was. I looked all around but couldn't find her. I figured that she would be back later.

I came back in the house and got Jason and Ashley ready for bed. I was then ready to turn in for the night myself. I again went outside to see if I could find Sarah. There was still no sign of her.

Hours later, Sarah came back to the house and marched straight into my room and woke me up.

"I'm back. But just so you know, I'm only doing this for Ellen and the kids."

"You wouldn't even have to be here if you would have listened to me in the first place!" I shouted at her.

Ashley began crying. I started to get out of bed.

"I'll do it. Stay in bed," Sarah told me.

I was awakened later that night by Jason jumping on my bed. "Wake up, Daddy!"

I sat up and rubbed my eyes. "What are you doing out of bed?" I asked him.

"There is somebody outside," he told me.

"No, there isn't. Go back to sleep."

"Can I sleep with you?" he asked.

"No, back in your own bed."

"No! No!" he shouted.

Just then, Sarah came rushing into my room. "Jason isn't in his bed!" she shouted.

Then she noticed Jason with me.

"What are you doing up?" she asked him.

"Auntie Sarah, there is somebody outside," he said.

Sarah looked at me. I got up out of bed and went outside to investigate. I went around the barn and through the yard and found no sign of anyone being out there. So I went back into the house. Sarah had put Jason back into bed and met me in the kitchen.

"Was there anybody out there?" she asked.

"No. Just as I figured, he was dreaming," I replied.

I went back to bed. Sarah decided to go out to do some investigating of her own. She went out and around the barnyard, taking in some deep breaths. She finally came back in the house and turned in for the night.

Then came the morning that I was heading out to other villages to try to find seed for the spring planting. I awoke before anyone else and got the wagon all packed up and ready to go. I went inside the house to grab a bite to eat. Sarah already had Jason eating at the table. She was holding Ashley.

"Benjamin, can you milk the goat before you leave?" she asked me.

"Why?" I snapped. "Are you to helpless to do it yourself?"

"Never mind, I'll do it myself!" she shouted back at me.

I didn't have anything to eat. I didn't even give Jason a hug before I left. I just wanted to be away from everything, especially Sarah. I couldn't stand being around her anymore.

I met with the others and we headed out. I looked back and could see Jason waving to me as I disappeared in the distance.

We had been in the wagon for an hour or so when I felt

the weight lift off of my shoulders. All the years of being the man of the village were now gone. It was just me and the guys; so far, I was liking it.

We were about a day's travel from the first village. The spring weather was approaching, and the streams had thawed. We decided to take some time and do some fishing. We parked the wagon and tied up the horses. We took our fly rods from the wagon and headed to the stream.

We spent several hours fishing. I didn't think of my family at all. We caught several fish, then decided to build a fire and camp by the stream that night

Sarah had her hands full back at the house. She was taking care of both kids and doing all the chores around the house. Since I decided not to ask anybody to help her, Sarah had Jason outside helping her milk the goat.

"Where did Daddy go?" he asked.

"He went on a trip," she told him.

"Did he go to Heaven too? Because he didn't tell me goodbye either."

"No, he'll be back in a few days. He had to get something for the village."

They finished milking the goat and took the milk up to the porch. Then they went to the woodpile and loaded some wood. They got back to the porch and Jason helped unload the wood.

"Thanks for your help, Jason," Sarah told him. "You make a good man of the house."

The guys and I were letting it all out. We got into the corn whiskey and were all pretty drunk. I liked the life even though it had been only a few hours. We drank and partied into the night.

In the morning, all of us were moving sluggishly. We

finally packed up camp and got on our way. We were all now technically single, so we decided to make a stop at a nearby village later that day to one of the guys' favorite old haunts.

We traveled into the evening and ended up in the village of Shanesville. We stopped at the local saloon, Shane's. There were people all around. We approached the bar.

"What can I get you boys tonight?" the bartender asked.

"Four beers," I told him.

We grabbed our beers and went out in the saloon to mingle. I couldn't help but notice some of the young ladies that were working at the bar.

"Look at her, Benjamin," Willie said to me.

I looked over at the young lady he was talking about and my mouth nearly hit the floor. I stared for a moment, and then she noticed me and waved me over to her. I got up from our table and went to sit with her.

"Where are you from, stranger?" she asked.

"A little village west of here," I answered.

"Do you have a name?"

"Oh, yes, Benjamin is my name."

"My name is Johanna."

I was so intrigued by her that I really wasn't paying attention when she told me her name.

"What brings you around here?" she asked.

"My friend Willie over there used to hang out here. We are on our way to Coalsville to see if we can get some seed for our village. We had a flood and it ruined almost all our crop from last season."

I went back to the bar and got another beer, then went back and spent more time with Johanna. The more time I spent with her, the more my urges were acting up.

She invited me back to her room in the bar, where she began to undress. She was in heat and I could smell it, and my animal side began to take over. I could hear her beating heart and smell her flesh. Her smell was so fresh; she was there for the taking.

All I could think of was Ellen.

"What's wrong, Benjamin?" she asked.

"It's not you, it's me. I need to get out of here."

She put her clothes back on and escorted me to the bar. I ordered Willie and Paul back to the wagon to rest for the journey in the morning.

Sarah had the kids in bed and was writing in her journal.

Benjamin blames me for Ellen's death. I don't know how much more of him I can stand right now. I'm only here because I know this is what Ellen would want. I just hope that when he comes home he has had time to cool off and think about it.

Sarah put her journal away in her nightstand and turned in for the night.

I slept off my drunken stupor. I woke Willie and Paul and we headed off to Coalsville. Willie and Paul were both silent the whole trip, which made the trip last forever.

We could soon see the edge of Coalsville. About ten minutes later we were there. We went into town and to the local saloon to get a bite to eat and find out who to talk to about getting some seed. I finally found a burly man named Jim Bob.

He told me, "You need to go see Mr. Stark at the general store. He should be able to help you out."

Willie, Paul, and I arrived at the general store and asked to speak to Mr. Stark.

"I'm Mr. Stark," the man behind the counter said. "How may I help you?"

"My name is Benjamin and this is Paul and Willie. We

traveled here from a little village west of here. Our harvest was flooded out this past season, and we are looking for seed we can plant this year to feed our village."

"I think I can help you out," Mr. Stark said. "What do you need?"

"We need enough corn and bean seed for almost three hundred acres," I said.

"Whoa, hold on a minute. You need enough seed for 300 acres?"

"Is there a problem?" I asked.

"I can only spare enough for one hundred acres of each, but if you travel farther east there is another village. There is a general store there owned by my brother. He should be able to finish out your order."

"We'll take what you can spare," I told him.

Mr. Stark walked over to a machine on his counter and punched some buttons on it. "That will be twenty dollars," he said.

I looked at him.

"Don't you have any money?" he asked.

"We do, but we were hoping to borrow the seed and return it from the harvest this fall," I said.

"I don't know you," Mr. Stark replied. "Why would I trust you with my livelihood? Giving you the seed and hoping you return some this fall is like not giving you the seed at all. One of our villages won't be able to eat. I don't risk my family like that. You boys need to leave before I call the sheriff."

"Call the sheriff," Willie shot back. "We haven't done anything."

"Get out of my store now or I'll get the sheriff," Mr. Stark repeated.

We left the general store empty-handed. I was discouraged; it seemed the further east we traveled, the less the people were like us back home. We headed back to the wagon in disgust.

"We should just take what we need and have some more fun before heading back," said Willie.

"We will do no such thing!" I shouted. We climbed into the wagon and headed out of the village.

"Where to next?" asked Paul.

I wanted to head for a different village, but I couldn't get Johanna out of my mind. "We're going back to Shanesville," I told them.

Chapter 24

Sarah was out finishing some chores while the kids were sleeping. She was approached by George.

"Is Benjamin around?" he asked.

"No, he went around to other villages to try to find some seed for planting this year. What do you need him for?" she said.

"No one has seen Josephine since Ellen's funeral and we were concerned. I know she has helped out in the past with the kids. I guess I was just wondering if you had seen her."

Sarah had to think for a moment. She had been so involved in doing everything around the house that hadn't even noticed what was going on around the village.

"As a matter of fact, I haven't seen her since the funeral either," she answered.

"If I get my wife to watch the kids, will you come with me to check on her?"

"I will," answered Sarah.

About twenty minutes later, there was a knock at the door. It was George and his wife Mildred. Sarah let them in and went over a few things with Mildred. Jason was up from his nap. Sarah went up to him.

"I'll be right back, buddy," she told him.

"Where you going?" he asked.

"I need to go with Uncle George to check on something."

Sarah gave him a kiss on his forehead and went with George over to Josephine's house.

"Are you and Benjamin going to raise the kids together?" George asked.

"I don't know," Sarah sighed. "Benjamin blames me for Ellen's death, and it makes me want to leave. But then I think of the conversation I had with Ellen when she told me that she appreciated everything I did for her family. That makes me want to stay."

"I was just wondering because Mildred and I have talked about taking the kids. Benjamin has too much responsibility to have the kids to deal with also."

"Why would you want to tear his family apart?" Sarah asked.

"We don't want to tear it apart. He is young and has too much on his plate. I just think the kids will be neglected if they stay with him."

Sarah was fuming inside. It seemed like George was trying to make her commit to staying with Benjamin.

They came to the fence surrounding Josephine's yard.

"Stop!" said Sarah.

"What for?" asked George.

Sarah took a deep breath. She looked at George but didn't say a word. They proceeded past the gate and in through the front door of the house.

"What happened here?" asked George.

Sarah said nothing. She kept her guard up and started looking around. Every room showed signs of a struggle. Sarah went into Josephine's bedroom and made a gruesome discovery. Josephine's body was torn to shreds. She fought to keep from gagging as she went to get George.

"Follow me," she told him.

George followed Sarah back into Josephine's bedroom.

"What the hell happened here?" he shouted.

"It looks like Elizabeth was here," replied Sarah.

"How could she do this?"

Sarah had to explain that Elizabeth must have gotten involved with a lycan when she went back to the village to find Laura and Charles.

"What is a lycan?" asked George

Sarah explained as the two of them went back into the village. They rounded up as many of the villagers as they could and met at the meeting building. Sarah stood in front of the villagers and told them what had happened to Josephine.

"A traitor has visited our village. She has danced with a lycan and now she is after revenge. The whole village is in danger."

"What do we do?" asked Kendall.

"We have to take turns guarding the village," Sarah replied. "One lycan can be overcome with weapons."

The men got together and made up a schedule for guarding the village. Sarah pulled George aside.

"Until Benjamin returns I want you and Mildred to take the kids. I can't take the chance of something happening to them. All the chores I've been doing make me leave them unattended."

George replied, "I think that is a good idea. You will be freed up to help with patrolling, then."

"That too," answered Sarah. "I think Elizabeth was out in front of the house the other night. Jason woke Benjamin up saying there was somebody outside his window. Benjamin went out and checked but couldn't find anything. I went out later and thought I smelled blood. That had to be the same night Josephine was murdered."

The meeting concluded and the villagers headed back to their homes and prepared for what they thought would be a fight.

Sarah and George walked into the house. George went right up to Jason.

"Hey, little guy, you're coming to stay with Aunt Mildred and me."

"I don't want to stay with you," Jason said. "I want to stay with Auntie Sarah."

George's postured changed.

"Boy, you're coming home with us, and that is final!" he shouted.

"Don't talk to him like that!" Sarah said.

"I'll do what I please. You just stay out of my business!"

George shoved Sarah to the ground and grabbed Jason and Mildred grabbed Ashley. They grabbed whatever they could fit in their hands and headed out the door. Sarah shook the cobwebs out of her head and headed out the door. She ran after George and Mildred but failed to see the hoe on the ground and tripped over it. When she got up she realized she couldn't put much pressure on her ankle. She hobbled back into the house.

I was living it up with the boys and Johanna. We were all pretty drunk.

"Do you want to see something amazing?" I asked Johanna.

"Yes, Benjamin, show me," she replied.

We left the bar and went to a secluded area. She started taking her clothes off and I moved in. We were really getting into it when I started thinking of Ellen again. I pushed Johanna away from me.

"Again?" she shouted. "Nobody turns me down!"

She grabbed me by the scruff of my shirt and pulled me back over to her. She climbed on top of me and began ripping my clothes off. I managed to throw her off. I was so frustrated by this time that I changed into a wolf. I turned, growled, and showed her my teeth. She turned and ran back toward the saloon screaming. I knew the others would be in trouble when she got back there. I ran in that direction.

Johanna ran into the saloon half naked. She pointed at Willie and Paul.

"Witches!" she shouted.

The crowd looked at the two of them. Before they knew it, the crowd was ambushing them. They were both too intoxicated to put up much of a battle. Knowing Willie, he was probably bragging about being a shape shifter anyway. They were tied up and taken to the center of town. The mayor had shown up.

"What's going on here?" he asked.

"Witches!" the crowd shouted.

"Who has proof of this?" the mayor asked.

"I do," Johanna said.

"Tell me, brothel girl."

She told the mayor and the crowd what she had seen.

You could hear the word "guilty" passed through the crowd. The mayor waited for a moment, then made his verdict.

"Burn them at the stake," he ordered.

I watched from a distance as the villagers gathered up wood. Willie and Paul were tied to a log and smaller sticks were laid around them.

"Benjamin!" echoed through the air.

The villagers lit the fire. I was ready to change and head down there to save my friends, but a gunshot from the crowd changed my mind. I sat back and watched them ignite the wood around my friends. I watched my friends burn alive for as long as I could stand to. Then, with a heavy weight on my heart, I changed into a wolf and headed back in the direction of home.

Chapter 25

Sarah had put the villagers in strategic places along the outskirts of the village. She was still fuming from the way George had treated her earlier. She took a deep breath, and then she thought of a plan.

Sarah went back to the house and began packing supplies into trunks. She took the trunks to the outskirts of the village and stashed them under some brush. She then returned to her post. She grew bored waiting for something to happen, so she changed into a wolf and headed out to investigate.

George had called another emergency meeting in the village.

"As of today I declare myself in charge of the village. I'm the new alpha of the pack. Benjamin failed at his job. Hell, he failed at his marriage. He couldn't control his wife. She killed my brother in cold blood. Benjamin hid that from all of you by feeding him to the hogs. He also lied to all of you about Laura, Charles, and Elizabeth. They are the beasts we now must fear. That wench that has been living with him is the cause of it all.

"He is supposed to be out getting seed for us, but the

boys he took with him told me different. He is out having fun while we sit here and wonder what our future holds. We were all doing well until he showed up."

Sarah stayed back and listened. She scanned the crowd and didn't see Jason or Mildred. So she headed to George's house. She knocked on the door, changed into a wolf, and waited for Mildred to answer. Sarah stayed quiet until Mildred came out to see who it was. Sarah then got between Mildred and the door so she couldn't get back in. She chased Mildred off the porch. Mildred went running for help.

Sarah went into the house and changed back into human form. She knew she wouldn't have long until Mildred found someone to come back with her to the house. Sarah grabbed Jason and took off through the backdoor. She ran as fast as she could, holding Jason.

Mildred's screams were finally answered. Luke came up to ask what was wrong.

"There's a wolf in my house and Jason and Ashley are both in there!" she screamed.

Luke ran back to his barn and grabbed a pitchfork. He and Mildred headed back to Mildred's house.

Sarah made it to the point in the woods where she had dropped off her belongings. She stopped to rest and put Jason down.

"You need to stay quiet, buddy," she told him. "They'll be looking for us."

Luke went in the house first. He looked around and didn't notice anything. He went back outside.

"Mildred, there is no wolf in your house," he said.

"The children!" she shouted. "We must check on the children!"

They went into the house together.

"Jason! Jason, are you here!" Mildred shouted.

There was no response. The two of them looked in each of the rooms. They found Ashley in the bassinette, but Jason was not in the house. Mildred grabbed Ashley, and she and Luke went to find George.

Sarah had rested and had made the decision not to try to go back for Ashley. She and Jason headed away from the village. Sarah took only what she could carry from her stash. They headed north.

George was just finishing his conversation with some of the villagers.

Mildred shouted, "George!"

George came running over to her. "What's going on, Mildred?" he asked.

"Jason is missing!" she told him.

"What do you mean, missing?" he asked.

The villagers George had been talking to gathered around the excitement.

"A wolf was at our house," Mildred said. "It tricked me and chased me away from the house. I found Luke, and when we went back to check on the kids, Jason was gone."

One of the villagers spoke up.

"They can't be too far," he said. "Let's get some more of us together and search."

"That's a good idea," replied George.

Sarah was beginning to tire, having to piggyback Jason, so the two of them stopped for a rest. Sarah found a clearing in the woods where she and Jason could have a little picnic.

The villagers were all back in the center of the village. George had filled them in on what had happened and he ordered them to split into groups and look for Jason. He even ordered the older kids to join in the search. The villagers split up into groups of six and headed out in all four directions. Smaller groups of three went between each group of six.

The search had been going on for about an hour when they stumbled upon Sarah's stash.

"It looks like someone was planning on staying here," said Luke.

They started to go through their find and noticed blankets and baby clothes in the trunk.

"They were planning on keeping a baby here also," stated Luke. "We have to go back and let George know about this."

Unfortunately for me, I was too close to the village trying to rest. I was in a deep sleep when I heard dead prairie grass being stomped on. I stayed quiet in my brush pile, not moving, because I expected the sounds might be hunters. Eventually the sounds passed. I came out of my brush pile and changed back into a human. I began my travel back to my village.

Luke and the others had arrived back at the village to inform George of what they had found.

"We found this in the woods about an hour's walk from here," Luke said.

"Bring that here," George told him.

George looked at the trunk, inspecting a marking on the outside of it. "So," he said, "she thinks she can outsmart me."

Luke gave George a confused look.

"Just as I thought. Sarah is behind this whole thing," declared George.

"It was a wolf," Mildred said. "Sarah was nowhere around."

"Shut it, woman," George told her. "You wouldn't understand if I told you anyway."

George knew the others would be back in an hour or so because of darkness, so he waited with his evidence in the center of the village for the others to arrive.

Sarah was concerned that she hadn't made enough progress for the day, so she planned on hiking as long as she could through the night. She packed up their things and headed out.

I was close enough to the village that I could smell smoke from the fires burning in the stoves to heat the houses. I was torn. I would be happy to see my kids, but I was depressed from coming back empty-handed.

I was at the outskirts of town when I noticed everyone gathered in the center of the village. I wondered what was going on. I ran right up to George.

"What's going on?" I asked.

"That wench that ruined your life has taken Jason and run off," he said.

"What do you mean?" I asked.

"What can't you understand? I said it in plain English. Your son is missing and your wench took him."

I knew Sarah wouldn't do anything like that, so I went to the house. I ran inside and saw that there were things thrown all over. I also noticed that Ellen's mother's trunk was missing. I looked all around but couldn't find anything.

I went back to George, who was waiting for me. He placed the trunk on the stump in front of him.

"See, Benjamin? Here is the proof."

I still had my doubts that Sarah had actually done what he was accusing her of.

"How do I know you didn't stage all of this?" I asked him. I should have kept my mouth shut.

"You stupid bastard," he replied. "Where is our seed? Where are Willie and Paul? Did you handle your task or did you fail at it, just like you do at everything else?"

This caught me off guard. Before I knew it, I was being subdued by three of the villagers. I struggled to get free but couldn't. Luke pointed a gun at my chest.

"Don't give me a reason to use this," he said.

I was ushered to Josephine's house. About 100 feet away I could smell the decaying flesh inside. It reminded me of the smell of our barn when I was younger. I struggled to get away, but the gun at my back convinced me not to try too hard. They pushed me into Josephine's house and back to her bedroom. I could see the pieces of her scattered all over the place. I put my head down.

"You brought all of this to our village," George said. "This plague you brought has done us more harm than good. You should have stayed away from here and not come back. You should have let nature take its course. Instead, you infected us with your curse. You killed your wife, her father, and my brother. You will not take from me again."

I had no reply. I myself wished that I hadn't cursed the village with what flowed in my blood. I just stood there. I had been blaming Sarah for everything when I should have been blaming myself.

I was escorted out of the house, tied to a fencepost, and forced to watch as Josephine's house was set on fire. The others left me tied to the post as the house burned. I figured they hoped the yard would catch on fire and burn me too.

The fire blazed and I was hot and sweaty. I was almost ready to pass out from the heat when I heard someone approaching.

"Poor Benjamin," a female voice said.

I recognized the voice as Mildred's. I turned and could see her coming up the lane. She stopped and put something down, then came up to me.

"Drink, Benjamin," she said as she put a jug to my lips.

I turned my head away.

"I'm on your side," she told me. "I don't want to hurt you."

I sniffed the jug and soon drank from it.

"We need to get you out of here," Mildred told me. "George has gone off his rocker and declared himself the new alpha of the village. He wants you dead, but he wants to do it in front of Sarah when they find her. He will torture you until they do."

She began untying me from the post.

"I have Ashley with me. I want you to see her before you leave. I will take good care of her. Sarah has Jason. She did it to protect him. She has always been there for you, Benjamin."

She finished untying me.

I went over to see Ashley, and gave her a big kiss. "Daddy loves you," I said.

I hugged Mildred.

"Thank you, Mildred," I told her as I ran off.

I made it out of the village. I changed back into a wolf and made a huge circle around the village, trying to track Sarah.

Mildred made it back to the house before George even knew she was gone. She was tending to Ashley when he walked in the door.

"Looks like it's going to be an early morning," he told her as he took off his coat.

"Why's that?" Mildred asked.

"Benjamin showed up tonight. Empty-handed, of course. I have to deal with him before we find that wench."

Mildred made no reply, just continued feeding Ashley.

Chapter 26

I finally tracked Sarah's scent and was on her trail. I was glad to find that Jason's scent was with hers. I knew they were safe, but I couldn't let George get away with his shenanigans. I decided I would lay low until later in the night, and then I would continue to track Sarah.

It was nearing 2:00 a.m. when I awoke to bloodcurdling howls and screaming. Then I heard some gunshots. I ran up to the outskirts of the village so I could see what was going on.

I saw the villagers in the fight of their lives. Three lycans were attacking the village. The villagers were scrambling all over the place. I knew that I would be in over my head if I entered the scramble, so I just stayed back and watched. Then I saw Mildred running with Ashley. I made my way toward her and held off a lycan so she could escape. I stayed far enough away that she wouldn't notice me. I watched her run off to safety. The lycans made short work of the men as they tried to defend their village.

Morning approached, and I knew the lycans soon would be settling in for the day. I decided to track Mildred instead of Sarah.

It didn't take long for me to catch up to Mildred. At her age, she couldn't travel very fast. She was sitting on a stump, holding Ashley and trying to catch her breath. I changed back into human form and approached her.

"Mildred, it's Benjamin. Are you okay?"

"Benjamin, is it really you?" she responded.

"Yes, Mildred, it's me." I came up to her so she could see me.

"What was that back there?" she asked.

"Those were lycans," I told her. "We need to get moving so they don't catch up."

"Just take Ashley and leave me here. I'm too old and will only slow you down."

I responded, "After you saved me, there is no way I will leave you here to be lycan food."

I gave her a few more minutes to rest and then we headed out.

Sarah finally made it to a village. She went to the first house she saw and knocked at the door.

A young woman answered. "How may I help you?"

"My son and I have been on our own in the wilderness for days. We need a place to stay and something to eat."

The young woman let Sarah and Jason into the house. "My name is Euclid. What's yours?" she asked.

Sarah replied, "My name is Sarah and this is my son Jason."

Euclid began warming some water up for Sarah and Jason to clean up. "What happened to you two?" she asked.

Sarah replied, "I had some issues with another villager and was forced out of the village."

Sarah bathed Jason as Euclid made something for them to eat. When Jason was clean, Sarah took him into the kitchen.

"Are you married, Euclid?" asked Sarah.

"I was married, but my husband just up and left. He came home from a hunting trip acting strangely. He left one morning without even saying goodbye," she answered.

Euclid staved off further questions by saying it was time to eat. Sarah dished up plates for Jason and herself. The room was quiet as they ate.

Mildred and I were on Sarah's trail. We had nothing to eat and no way to feed Ashley. We needed to find a village as soon as possible. We found a clean stream and I ripped off some of my shirt. We submerged the piece of cloth in the stream and let Ashley suck the water from it.

"This won't do for long," said Mildred.

Mildred wasn't lying. Ashley grew tired of water as her little tummy rumbled. We decided to break away from Sarah's path and try to find a village for Ashley's sake.

Sarah put Jason down for a nap and then sat back down at the table with Euclid.

"Thank you so much for your hospitality," said Sarah.

Euclid replied, "I don't get much company. Ever since my husband left, I've been removed from the village. I have rations enough for a year and then I don't know what I'm going to do."

"I can help you," Sarah said.

"How do you plan on doing that?"

"I've lived alone almost all of my life. I'm pretty good at farming, so if we can stay with you, I'll help you out."

"Let me think about it."

Mildred and I approached a village.

"You take Ashley and go," I told Mildred.

"Are you sure?" asked Mildred.

"Yes, I'm sure. I have things I need to tend to."

I left Mildred and Ashley. I watched them as they went into the village. After they disappeared, I set my sights on going back to my home village. I knew Sarah and Jason were safe and Mildred and Ashley were safe. Now I wanted to make sure George was put in his place.

When I arrived, the carnage was unbelievable. There were decaying bodies all around. I looked through all the houses until I found what I was looking for. Clinging to his last bit of life, George was lying in his barn.

"Help me, Benjamin," he struggled to say.

"Why would I want to help you? You condemned me in my own village. You chased my family away. You came between Sarah and me, and you fueled my doubt about her and her intentions. So, tell me, why would I save you?"

I grabbed him by the scruff of his shirt.

"Do it, Benjamin! Do it!" he shouted.

I wanted to kill him, but I held my cool.

"You stupid bastard. Lester didn't try to kill Ellen. I did!"

I dropped him and backed way.

"Change, Benjamin. Kill me. You'll be no better than him!" he shouted.

George pointed. In the dim light I could make out a figure. Ryan was standing in the barn with George and me. Suddenly I felt something hit the back of my head and I passed out.

When I came to, I was caged like an animal. I looked all over myself to make sure I hadn't been bitten or scratched. As my head cleared, I could see Ryan sitting in a chair across from me.

"What do you want from me?" I shouted.

"What do I want from you? Let's see," he replied. "I

want you dead, I want your kids, and I want Sarah. But I'm willing to make you a deal."

"What's your deal?" I asked.

"I want your little girl, and I'll leave you alone," he said.

"Why do you want her for?" I asked.

"Her blood," he answered. "I'm sick, Ashley is dead, and in fact my whole clan is dead. She is the only person that can save me."

"Why would I want to save you?"

"I'm the only one that can stop what stalks you. I didn't attack your village; it was one of my mistakes. I've rediscovered my feelings and found a way to control myself. I made a mistake one night and changed a man that reminded me of myself when I was younger, full of piss and vinegar. I was hoping he would take my place before the sickness took me. He is the one who attacked the village and your friends."

"You killed my family. Why would I trust you?"

"That's how we became sick. Your family's clan was on the verge of starvation and infected with scarlet fever when we killed them. We did them a favor. We ended their suffering."

"I don't know if I can sacrifice my daughter to you. Is there any other solution?" I asked.

Ryan began coughing.

"No, there isn't," he said finally. "Either save me so I can finish what I started, or live on the run. They will track your kind down and kill them."

"You said you need her blood. Will you kill her?"

"I should be able to feed on her blood for a few days and slowly heal, but if I don't get enough time, I will have to kill her."

I had no other choice. If Ryan weren't serious, he

would have killed me when he had the chance.

"I'll do it," I said.

Ryan got up out of his chair and let me out of the cage. He shook my hand.

"Thank you," he said.

The two of us went over to George. Ryan changed into a lycan and finished him off. I was disappointed that I couldn't do it myself, but the consequences if I had made me feel better about Ryan doing it.

I peered into the lycan's eyes. As Ryan had said, there were feelings there; they weren't just black and emotionless.

Ryan changed back into human form and the two of us headed to the village where Mildred and Ashley were. On the way, Ryan told me to kill him after he finished his business. He looked me in the eyes.

"Promise me that," he said.

"I promise," I said.

We arrived at the village and found Mildred and Ashley. I had to convince Mildred of what Ryan wanted to do with Ashley. We went to the local doctor and asked if he could bleed Ashley. We told him she was sick and we thought her blood needed to be replaced. With some convincing and a promise to be quiet, he agreed to do it.

Every day we brought Ashley to his office to have blood taken from her. Ryan grew stronger each day.

I left that village to find Sarah. When I did, she informed me that she wanted nothing to do with Ryan. I took her out on a walk and talked to her.

"I'm sorry, Sarah," I said. "I had no business treating you the way I did. I should've known that you would do anything for my family. I wish we could start over."

"Benjamin, I want to start over with you. You do what you need to do with Ryan. Come back and find me when you are done. Jason and I will look forward to seeing you."

Sarah gave me a hug and a kiss on the porch of Euclid's house.

"Good luck," she told me.

I returned to find that Ryan had taken a turn for the worse. Now I had a big decision: sacrifice my daughter, or live a life on the run. I walked into the barn and approached Ryan.

"What should I do?" I asked.

Ryan answered, "Change and kill me."

"Why would I want to do that? Won't I become a lycan?" I asked.

"No. You'll be like me. You'll have feelings but all the power," he said.

My confusion must have shown on my face, because Ryan spoke up again.

"You'll be the same person. Just take wolfsbane and you will have a normal life. But don't do it with anger or thoughts of revenge. Clear your mind of anything I've done to you in the past. Don't think of it as getting even. Those thoughts will make you uncontrollable."

I sat back and pictured me and my family. That cleared my mind. Then I changed and savaged Ryan. The rush was exhilarating. I felt the power running through my veins.

I backed away. I changed back into human form in time to hear his last words.

"Thank you," he said.

To my surprise, he hadn't been lying. His statement made me feel good inside. I still could feel.

I cleaned up, then went in and passed the news on that Ryan was dead. Mildred was relieved. She was weary of all the trips to the doctor to bleed Ashley. I told her I would be leaving in the morning to get Sarah and Jason.

Chapter 27

In the morning, I felt stronger and more alert than I ever had. I left before anyone else was awake. When I changed into a wolf, I was bigger and stronger than I had been. I found that I covered ground much faster. I could hear and smell much better than before.

I made it to the village where Sarah and Jason were. I knocked on Euclid's door and was greeted by Sarah.

"What's with you?" she asked. "I could smell you a mile away."

"I killed Ryan," I told her.

"Why?"

I told her how he had grown sicker, and about the conversation we had.

"He figured it out," she said.

"Figured what out?" I asked.

"It had to do with the way your family came to be shape shifters," she said. "That's why he needed Ashley your sister and Ashley your daughter. Their bloodline. I can't believe I didn't think of that."

Things were beginning to make sense to me. That's why Ryan had despised me as a child: because of my bloodline. He knew I would become the alpha over him.

Jason ran out and gave me a big hug. "Are we going home, Daddy?" he asked.

"Soon," I told him.

I looked at Sarah. "I have some unfinished business to tend to. I would like to bring Mildred and Ashley up here to stay, if it is all right with Euclid."

Sarah responded, "I should go with you back to Mildred. I think your unfinished business began here."

"What do you mean?"

"I'll explain on the way," she said.

Sarah gathered up Jason and her things. She thanked Euclid for her hospitality and told her she would keep her promise and come back to help her farm. We headed out.

Sarah waited until we took a break to let Jason nap before she explained.

"I think Euclid's husband is the cause of your problem," she said.

"What makes you think that?"

"He began acting strangely. He took off, and she hasn't seen him since. She described his actions, and they were similar to what you told me about when your parents changed."

"So why would he be the root of my problem?"

"I saw a sketching of him. It's Brian, the man who assaulted Laura."

"Wait a minute," I said. "The path they're taking will bring them right back here. Laura and Elizabeth will be ordered to take care of Euclid."

"Right," Sarah said, "and any village in their way will be ravaged just like ours was. You need to put an end to it. I wish I could help you."

I had to take time and think. The way Sarah put it made me feel uneasy, I had all the powers but no experience in using them. I became very quiet.

"What's on your mind, Benjamin?" asked Sarah.

"It should be you," I said.

"What do you mean, it should be me?"

"You have a lot of knowledge and experience. I'm new at this. I hope I don't let us down."

"Benjamin, it has to be you. You weren't born with this curse; it was given to you. Whether you want it or not, your bloodline controls our destiny."

"What do I do?" I asked.

"Do what comes naturally. Do your best. You always seem to weasel your way out of situations," she said.

It was time to get Jason up and continue our journey to rejoin Mildred.

Mildred was tending to Ashley when we showed up. Sarah went right over to Mildred and took Ashley away from her.

"I've missed you, little girl," she said as she kissed Ashley's forehead.

We sat Mildred down and told her what was going on.

"I want you and Sarah to take the children far away from here," I told her. "I'm sure whoever attacked our village will track us here. I'm surprised they haven't been here yet."

"But where will we go?" she asked.

"Sarah will take you there. Only she and I know where it is. We want to keep it secret."

"But I like it here. Why can't I stay here?" she asked.

"Sarah needs your help with the kids. If you won't do it for Sarah or yourself, do it for the kids."

Mildred finally agreed to leave with Sarah in the morning. The kids stayed with her while Sarah and I guarded the village. For hours we walked back and forth, and neither of us smelled anything. Sarah decided she should turn in for the night, so we changed back into human form and headed back into the village.

Sarah found a comfortable spot to sleep and I stood guard. I looked down at her as she slept and realized how lucky I was that she was still with me. Through it all, she stood by my side. I decided right then that, if I survived my mission, I would give her what she had always wanted.

I watched Sarah until the sun began to rise. She got up and stretched.

"Have you been up all night?" she asked me.

"I couldn't sleep," I said. "I have too much on my mind. You should get ready to go."

Sarah gathered Mildred and the kids. They stopped to say goodbye as they left. I hugged Jason.

"I love you, buddy," I told him.

"I love you too, Daddy."

I kissed Ashley on the forehead.

"I love you, baby," I said to her.

Finally, I gave Sarah a hug. "Thank you. I owe you so much. I will make it up to you when I return," I told her.

They headed out. I watched them until I couldn't see them anymore. Then I headed out myself.

The next day I arrived at the village where Sarah had met Euclid. I kept my distance so I wouldn't cause any problems. I missed my family dearly, and the words that Ryan said ran through my head: my bloodline was the only thing that could end the problem. I wanted to end the curse, but I wasn't looking forward to the altercation. How could I kill Elizabeth or Laura? I had changed them when they were so young. I had to think of Ellen. They didn't take into consideration that she had a family before they killed her. The more I stewed on that, the angrier I became.

The days passed. I could only assume that Sarah had

safely made it where she was going. Spring was here, and normally I would be in the fields planting at this time. I was enjoying the sunset when I heard something in the distance.

As the sunset and the daylight disappeared, the howling grew louder and louder. The villagers heard it also. The men locked their families up in their houses and prepared for a fight. I went to the center of the village and joined the gathering.

"Who are you?" one of the villagers asked.

"I don't have time to explain right now. You all are no match for what's coming. They want Euclid. You all need to be with your families. Stay inside and don't interfere," I said.

The men were confused. They didn't know who I was or why was I telling them what to do. It didn't take long for them to scurry once they saw what they were up against, though.

The three lycans appeared from the brush. The men scattered. I stood my ground and was soon joined by Euclid. I guess she knew more than Sarah led me to believe. She stood beside me as the lycans approached.

"We're over here!" I shouted.

"Brian, it's me!" Euclid yelled.

"Look what I have!" I shouted as I grabbed Euclid.

The male lycan gave us his full attention. The female lycans let out a big howl and began to charge us. I knew they were after Euclid, so I threw her out of the way before I changed. I finished changing just as the females approached. I knocked the first one off to the side. The second one then charged me. I had a clear shot at her throat and didn't miss. I tore her trachea out in one bite. Then I turned my attention back to the first female. She had cleared the cobwebs out of her head. She snarled at me as she approached. I was able to knock her on her back and tear her trachea out as well.

The male was so distracted by Euclid that he had held his position. Now he realized he was alone.

I approached him. He stood his ground and began showing his fangs. As I got closer I could feel the testosterone in the air. I knew I was in for a battle.

I lunged at him. He moved out of the way, knocking me to the ground. He jumped on me and we began to roll around, fighting. All the commotion was drawing a crowd. The villagers gathered around to watch us fight. Soon the lycan broke free and tried to go after Euclid. A gunshot from the crowd clipped one of his legs and stopped him short.

Crippled but not dead, the lycan became enraged. His testosterone levels had risen to a high level. He jumped back into the battle with me. He hit me as I was recovering. I took several bite wounds on my body.

I was beginning to give up until I thought of my family. That gave me the energy for another strike. I lunged at his throat; at the same time, I felt something hit my chest. It burned. I let out a yelp as I fell to the ground in pain.

The lycan stood over me. I covered my throat as well as I could. I could envision him destroying my family.

As he toyed with me in victory, I mustered the energy for one last attempt. I could feel his blood flowing through my teeth as I ripped and tore. I didn't even know where I got him, but as I blanked out, I felt his heart stop beating. I had won, but everything was dark.

Sarah and Mildred were concerned because I hadn't joined them.

"We need to find him," Sarah said.

"I agree," said Mildred.

They found a wagon they could borrow and set out on their way.

"Benjamin! Oh, no, Benjamin, wake up!"

I fought to open my eyes. I didn't recognize where I was. I blinked to clear my eyes, and I saw a blurry vision of Sarah.

"Is it really you?" I struggled to ask.

"Yes, Benjamin, it's me," she said.

"Did I finish it?"

"You did."

"Is Jason with you?" I asked.

"He doesn't need to see you like this," she said. "Take time and heal."

"I'm not going to heal," I told her.

"Benjamin, don't say that. You're going to be all right. You can't leave us. You made me a promise." Tears formed in her eyes.

"I'm sorry," I replied. "I know I promised you that we would be a family. Ellen wants you to raise the kids. I'm going to join her. Please go get Jason."

Sarah finally went to get Jason. He came into the room and could tell I wasn't doing well.

"Hi, buddy," I struggled to tell him.

"Daddy, are you okay?" he asked.

"Daddy is going to be with Mommy. You are the man of the house now. Take care of Sarah and Ashley."

He crawled up on the bed and wrapped his arms around me.

"I love you, Daddy. Tell Mommy I miss her."

Jason had accepted my death. Sarah was having difficulties.

"Damn it, Benjamin, hold on for me. I want to share my life with you," she cried.

With my last words, I told Sarah I loved her too, and that she would make a great mother to my children. Sarah was holding my hand as I took my last breath.

Epilogue

May 1, 1897:

Today was Benjamin's funeral. It was small, just as he would have wanted it. I honored his request for Jason. It was hard to get Jason to do it, but it is vital for his future that he have the same genetic mutation that Ryan passed on to Benjamin. I'm saddened by all the tragedy I have endured in the last year, but I have to be strong for Jason and Ashley's sake. I hope they adjust well and lend a helping hand as Euclid and I begin our new adventure. I don't think I could ever feel for another man what I did for Benjamin.

May 1, 1900:

Benjamin has been gone for three years now. The kids are growing up well. Jason is a spitting image of Benjamin and Ashley favors her mother. I have learned a lot raising these kids. I moved us all west to Minnesota. We are able to write a new chapter here. Jason has reached puberty, and I have struggled to control him. I'm glad for the wolfsbane. Ashley is a sweet young girl. I'm sure Benjamin and Ellen are smiling down upon us.

Jeremy Wenning is a Graduate of Celina High School, Celina OH. He resides in Coldwater, OH with his wife Vickie, of 13 years, two daughters, Brianna & Lauren and two Chocolate Labs (Coco & Pebbles). He is an entrepreneur and works for Mercer Health transport squad. In Jeremy's spare time, he enjoys writing & hunting, volunteers for the local emergency squad and coaches softball.